D0112481

Quiet
Amish
Courage

By Samuel Byler and
Linda Byler-Sortor

Desert Shadow Books LLC
Phoenix, Ariz.

QUIET AMISH COURAGE

Copyright Samuel Byler and Linda Byler-Sortor, 2013

Desert Shadow Books LLC
Phoenix, Ariz.

ISBN 978-0-615-83208-1

Cover design by Mark Middleton

Manufactured in the United States of America
First printing May 2013

ACKNOWLEDGEMENTS

Sam and Linda would like to thank a few of the people who helped make this book possible.

A special thank you to all our family and friends who were so supportive. You believed in us and we are so grateful.

To Mark Middleton with HitAGap Signs and Designs for the beautiful cover. We knew what we wanted and you delivered.

Jason Mackenzie of Supernatural Photography for your photography skills. You are greatly appreciated.

A special thank you to Rob Bignell of Inventing Reality Editing Services. You not only did a great job of editing but your kind words were inspiring and encouraging.

Prologue

She crept out of bed and put her head against the door. Turning the knob slowly, she opened it just far enough to hear the muffled voices of her parents coming up the short hallway from their bedroom. Her mother sounded anxious as she pleaded with her father. "Please Will, What are we going to do? We can't keep living like this, it's no way for a child to live. I want her memories to be more than this." Her father replied in a deep inaudible voice, a low rumble she couldn't distinguish. Her heart pounded as she listened to her mother make her case.

Her mother continued, her voice anguished, "She views the Bontragers as more her family than she does us. I've wondered if she doesn't just wish we'd leave her there."

She didn't have to strain anymore to hear her father as he clearly stated in a frustrated tone, "Oh for goodness sake, Malinda, just stop, there is nothing we can do or change about our situation. All we can do is keep her safe. Now, is not the time to tell anyone."

The young girl strained to hear more but the voices stopped and she knew her parents were settling in for sleep. She noiselessly went back to bed, hoping the dreams wouldn't come back to haunt her. Waking her from sleep so many times she had dreaded night's arrival.

But they hadn't come in a while now and she hoped they were gone for good. The conversation she'd overheard faded as she thought of the next day, knowing she would be with the Amish family with whom she always felt so secure. There, she had found a happiness that never seemed attainable at home. Her parents were never unkind to her, but living with a mother who seemed to always be in a crisis or a father who never seemed present made her life lonely.

It seemed like she had just gone to sleep when she felt her father shaking her awake, her mother was frantically digging clothes out of her dresser drawer. "Wake up Sylvia, he said, we have to leave." She sat up rubbing her eyes. "Hurry, go to the bathroom and quickly get dressed.

And then she remembered, this was her nightmare coming alive. It wasn't just a dream that was about to happen but one that had happened before.

Chapter 1

He looked out over the classroom, eight grades in all, looking back at him. Solemn eyes with a questioning stare, wondering what he would be like as a teacher. The small one-room schoolhouse held enough space for 43 students, but this year's enrollment was 37, leaving room for a few more.

He wondered why he had ever thought he could undertake this task, but the thought of going back to what he had left behind filled him with more dread than the thought of the next nine months facing the children. The front row held the four small first graders and the upper grades were in the back of the room. The school had a reputation for being a more difficult one to teach, and that didn't help the butterflies already making havoc in his stomach. His teacher's aide sat across the room from him at her desk, smiling like she had no fear at all, her face serene as she surveyed the room and glanced at the faces.

He cleared his throat. "Good morning children, my name is Allen; you may call me Teacher Allen." The formal title of teacher being almost difficult to say. "And this is Teacher Ada..." He pointed to the aide. "I have never done this before, but if we all work together, and try to get along, we should all do great."

The back of the school twittered a bit as if to say "wanna bet?" His stomach wrenched as he remembered his own youth, and in a rush, he knew if there was a payback, he would live to regret his own last several years in school.

He had come to Ohio from Michigan to teach when he had heard they were seeking a teacher. They had wanted to look outside the community, thinking the children may respond better to never having known the teacher, thus making them seem less like a peer but more of an authority figure.

He had mentioned the subject to his parents, and they seemed to think it would be a good idea. Almost a year away may be what he needed to work through his grief and somehow put a life back together again.

So he had written them letting them know of his interest and was shocked when he had received the acceptance letter asking him to indeed teach their school.

He was staying in a small empty add-on to a house that was to be the Dawdy Haus when the intended grandparents were old enough to downsize and move in. The house was small and just the right size for a single person or a couple. It was included in his salary along with the wood for winter. He wasn't much of a cook, but so far that didn't seem to be a problem since he had lots of people dropping off containers of food. His icebox was about ready to overflow with the meals given.. The food was good, almost as good as his mom's cooking. But nothing beat your own mother's cooking. He had heard it took about a year for a married man to adjust to his wife's cooking and not long for his mother's meals.

He took the roll call and asked them to stand and recite the Lord's Prayer in German. They all sat back down and reached for their songbooks. As custom in every Amish school, two to three songs were sung. They were chosen by order of turn, each child choosing a song and leading it until over a period of days all had their turn, and then it began all over again.

The first song chosen was "Amazing Grace," and he somehow found it appropriate. "A good way to start off a new year; it will take a whole lot of grace to get me through this," he thought wryly.

The notes of the last song faded. He went to the blackboard and began to assign classes.

He remembered how his own teachers had done it, but looking back it had all seemed so easy. Now he understood the skill and efficiency it took to make a room with eight grades succeed.

Ada moved to the first grader's row of desks, telling them to get out certain books and getting them started before moving on to the second grade. He couldn't help but notice the kindness in her tone as she spoke to each child, speaking as each one mattered as much as the other. "She is a natural for this, and she sure seems to like children," he thought as he wrote on the board.

The morning moved on quickly, and before he knew it, the time to dismiss for noon had arrived.

The room was finally quiet as the last of the students had left, noisily rushing out the doors and home to tell parents all about the day. Allen sat at his desk, his head spinning a little bit but with a pleased look on his face. "All in all the day went fairly well, what do you think?" he asked Ada Marie.

Ada Marie looked up from the papers she was grading

and smiled, "Yes, I would agree with you," she said. "Well," he said, gathering up his papers and putting them into his leather satchel, "If you don't mind, I think I'll go on home and finish this work there."

"Sounds like a good idea, she said, I'll be heading home soon myself."

Allen hesitated, "You will make sure to lock up?" "Of course, you have a great evening and see you tomorrow."

"You as well," he said, as he put on his hat and picked up his satchel to leave for the half-mile walk home.

He strolled out the driveway of the small school, noting how the corn tassels in the field across the road were darkened and beginning to dry. Summer is going to end soon, he thought, and then I won't have such a nice warm walk home, so I may as well enjoy it while I can. Amos Raber's medium-sized brown dog came running up to him as he walked in their driveway. Allen liked dogs; cats he wasn't so sure about. "Hey boy, he said to the dog. Did you have a good day?" The dog wagged his tail and squirmed as if to say "Of course, but even better now that I get to see you."

Little Anna stood on the front porch, looking at him as he walked past on the sidewalk leading around the side of the house toward the Dawdy Haus on the back side. He smiled at her. She was a student in her first year. Ada Marie had jokingly told him the day before, when they were at the school preparing for the first day, that talk was, "Anna thinks she will be a teacher's pet since you live at her house." He had laughed then and looking at her now he asked, "How did you like your first day?"

Anna got a big smile on her face, and she shyly ducked

her head a little bit and said in a quiet voice. "Fine."

He smiled and went on to his house. He unlocked the door and entered the still and quiet house. The dark curtains hung closed from when he had closed them the night before. Crossing the room he pushed them back. The windows looked out across a pasture with a creek in the background, also serving as a foreground to the woods. The view was nothing to complain about. "I think this place will do," he thought.

The room was square with an ell shape on the back side where the kitchen was located; the table was sitting to the side, giving the living room a large space. The stove sat in the corner, the wood box empty and waiting to be filled for the long winter ahead. His bedroom was on the right, and the bathroom was in a small room off it. He placed his satchel on the table that would serve as his desk for the next nine months and sat down on one of the chairs. Looking around the room, he wondered if he would be able to stand the quiet for so long. Although he had grown up as an only child, for so many years he at least had his parents to talk to. He pulled out the contents of the satchel, and began stacking the papers in the appropriate piles by each grade. He smiled as he looked at the first graders' drawings. He had looked forward to having children of his own. And as scary as it seemed, he had wanted a minimum of four, and possibly more, if the Lord intended. He held one drawing in particular, smiling as he thought of Billy, the mischievous looking six year old who always seemed on the verge of doing something naughty.

The picture was of a horse, its head hanging over a

fence with a blob, which he assumed was a dog, looking up at him. Allen worked steadily for an hour and a half, stopping when he felt a rumbling in his stomach. He rose and went to the icebox, opening the door he looked in, a jumble of plastic containers arranged inside. Opening one with a red lid, he saw what looked like meatloaf. Setting it on the counter, he looked for other things to go along with it and found green beans and what he thought was scalloped potatoes. He placed them in a baking dish and lit the oven. The stove was operated with kerosene, and he waited for it to heat up enough to place the dish inside.

Chapter 2

Growing up, Allen read voraciously about the world outside his small Amish community.

Knowing that the choice he was planning on making intended for him to never leave but would bind him to the Amish church forever. He really never gave leaving his heritage much thought. He liked the stability it gave him and sense of belonging.

He had friends with whom he had grown up with who chafed under the authority of the church. Even though they were now members of the church, he knew they still struggled.

He guessed the oven was hot enough. He knew that somehow he was going to need to learn more about cooking. Soon enough the meals would stop coming as the newness of him being there would wear off and the meals coming in would not be so plentiful. As the Amish did not have electricity, he knew that ready-made meals for a microwave oven were not a choice either. "I could, however, eat soup," he thought. That only needed a can opener and a small pot. He sat on the recliner and dug in the magazine rack that was part of the stand beside the chair. Finding a Reader's Digest, he flipped through it looking for "Enrich Your Word Power." He loved learning new words and had always made it mandatory to speak with proper grammar. He had often heard in his life that he didn't have an accent like so many of his friends. Finding what he was looking for, he started the puzzle. Twenty minutes later, he graded himself and was pleased to know he had only three incorrect. "Next time I'll do better," he promised himself. He looked at the clock and smelled the food in the oven. He rose, making his way to the sink where he washed up in preparation to eat.

Pulling the food out of the oven, he carefully set it on the hot pad. Dishing it out on a plate, he moved to the table after pouring himself a glass of water. Seating himself at the same chair he had sat earlier, he bowed his head and gave thanks and ate. Chewing his food, he thought back over the events that had brought him here, causing him to leave his parents and the community that was so familiar to him. Sadness, once again, rushed over him as he realized how much he had lost.

Married for only a year and a half, all his hopes and dreams crushed in one moment. He would never forget the blow of first learning that his beloved Sarah Ann had died.

He had been spending the day with his father at an auction, one he had looked forward to going to as soon he had heard about it. That morning was beautiful, not a day you'd wake up to and imagine that your life would take such a drastic change.

He and his father had left in a wagon in the event they found things too large to haul home in a buggy. Since they were newlyweds and living upstairs in his parents' home, he and Sarah Ann needed more than just a few items yet to fill their own home. Since the items listed were more along the way of things for the basement and barn, she didn't feel the need to go along. "Were it an icebox or washing machine I'd be going, or more importantly a couch or chair," she had stated when reading over the advertisement from the paper. "You go and enjoy the day with your father, and I'll go to town to get a few things I need." They lived only a mile and a half from the local store that had mostly everything they needed, and Sarah Ann walked there pulling a wagon. She never saw the car bearing down on her until it was too late. A hit and run. He had often wondered what her last thoughts were. Did she know what was about to happen? His eyes filled with tears as the hopelessness again washed over him. He struggled with the loneliness that filled him with an ache that didn't seem able to be satisfied. He finished the last of the food and thought of how much better it would have been if had been fresh and not reheated but pushed that thought aside as he realized that he needed to be grateful for the kindness he had been shown.

He washed the few dishes, dried and put them away. Ignoring the rack that was under the sink. Sarah Ann had always said the rack was for busy mothers or lazy people and that dishes didn't belong on the counter, dirty or not. That was one thing he had liked and disliked about her – liked that she loved cleanliness and disliked that the times he felt like just sitting and talking he had to almost pull her down beside him so she'd leave some chore.

He cherished the many talks they'd had together. Talking came easily for them. She was one person he felt safe opening up to, and they had spent many evenings just sharing. She was a little more guarded about herself, and he didn't know all that much about her family. He only knew she was raised by an elderly aunt in Holmes County. When the time came to be married, she asked to not have a large wedding but a quiet one in the Sunday morning service. He had found that a bit odd, since he thought every girl dreamed of a big wedding. But he had agreed.

His mother had fallen in love with Sarah Ann from the beginning, liking her friendliness and her never ending cheerfulness. She hadn't lost a son but gained a daughter, and Allen knew how fortunate he was by his mother's attitude. Many a daughter-in-law didn't acquire the mother-in-law that Sarah Ann found and Allen knew his mother grieved Sarah Ann like she would have had it been her own child. He also knew his father grieved. In one of the rare times he saw his father show emotion, just before the funeral, his father had laid his hand on his shoulder and said in a broken voice, "We will get through this somehow." Among most Amish men, it wasn't customary to hug others.

Allen sighed and pushed the thoughts away, brushing his eyes with his hands. He knew dwelling on the pain did nothing to relieve it, but getting busy with something would.

He went outside and saw Amos and his sons working on a woodpile that was freshly cut and ready to be stacked in the woodshed. Going over to them, he offered his services, and for the next several hours he helped fill and haul a wheelbarrow and making numerous trips back and forth.

Amos's wife, Saloma, brought them some lemonade

and fresh sugar cookies while they took a short break. They sat making small talk while devouring the soft homemade cookies.

They stopped just before dark, and Allen headed into the house to clean up and open a book that he had thought looked promising. He spent the next two hours reading and when he found himself yawning and finding it difficult to stay awake, put down the book and went to bed. As he lay there, he realized that the day had not been as bad as he had feared, and found himself looking forward to the next morning and the challenges that lay before him.

Allen woke the next morning to rain drumming on the roof. He lay for a while listening, remembering how as a boy he'd be glad to hear the rain since they worked outside he'd get a break from spending the day laboring in his father's masonry business. He rose and went to the sink, looking at himself in the mirror. He supposed that as far as looks go, he wasn't too frightening. His thick brown hair was healthy and didn't seem to be in imminent danger of falling out. He had a beard as required by a married Amish man but bent the rules somewhat by keeping it neatly trimmed. His nose was nice and straight, brown eyes and his teeth were not too bad, he thought. He looked at the one crooked tooth that had always bothered him, but Sarah Ann had told him she thought it gave him character. He stood just over six feet tall, his body lean from all the hard work he had put it through.

He brushed his teeth and got dressed for the day. "Cereal sounds like a good idea," he thought, since he remembered seeing some in the cupboard. He went to the kitchen and ate his breakfast, wondering if there may be an umbrella in the pantry or back entryway. Rinsing out his bowl, he left it in the sink and went looking for the umbrella. He found one hanging on a hook in the back entry that also contained a washing machine and the water pump that pumped his water. He noticed that he'd soon be needing some white gas and made a mental note to remember to ask Amos where it was kept. He went back inside and remembered that he had forgotten all about preparing a lunch. He hurriedly tossed together a sandwich and some pretzels left over from the drive from his parents. "I really need to make a trip to the grocery store very soon," he thought.

Grabbing his satchel, umbrella and lunch bag he went out the door. The rain was coming down in sheets, the wind catching the umbrella. He carefully held the umbrella so it wouldn't get caught up in the wind and bending his head he made his way out the driveway.

He hurried up the road to the school, arriving just before Ada Marie. Her face reflected a sunny personality, as if to tell the rain that it couldn't keep that from her. Her cheery "Good morning" sounded in the still room, and he smiled at her as returning the greeting.

They both prepared for their day as they waited for the children to arrive. Ada Marie hummed quietly as she looked through books, readying her lessons for each class she was assigned to.

Allen was glad the silence between them was comfortable. Some people never seemed to like silence and thought they had to constantly be talking, but he sensed that with Ada Marie she didn't mind the quiet.

The children began arriving and soon the room was filled with noise. Promptly at 8:45, Allen rang the bell, and the children all filed to their desks to begin another day. The morning wore on as Allen and Ada Marie worked together setting out lessons and answering hands raised with questions. Noon came, and after the children were dismissed for recess, they were alone once again. She asked if he was settling in and he replied that he was.

Ada Marie asked if he was interested in helping organize something to put around the wall near the ceiling and if he had any thoughts on a fall scene to be put on a large bulletin board. He tentatively suggested that maybe the small children could draw something for the wall and the upper grade girls could do the bulletin board. Allen realized that he may be in way over his head. This didn't involve how many bricks it required to do a fireplace or how much concrete for a garage floor. He laughingly said, "I should have paid more attention to these things when I was in school."

Ada Marie laughed and said, "As a boy, you really weren't expected to be too interested."

The bell rang, bringing the children back in for the afternoon studies. The afternoon went quickly, and it was time for another day to end.

Allen trudged home, dread at facing another evening home alone, foremost in his mind. He walked in the driveway, and once again, Sammy the dog greeted and jumped alongside him as he made his way to the door.

Setting his satchel and umbrella on the table, he took off his hat and sat down. There was a knock, and he opened the door to find Saloma standing there with letter in her hand.

"This came today and I needed to sign for it," she said. "They said it required a signature confirmation, but it was okay if I signed for you. I hope that was fine."

He reassured her that indeed it was, and she left. He closed the door and looked at the envelope. It looked official, the return address listed as Wooster, Ohio. He opened the letter, and it in turn contained a sealed envelope. As he looked at the sealed envelope, he wondered, "Why would this be sent to me?"

He opened the envelope, and a key fell out. He pulled out a handwritten page and a photo.

He looked at the photo and in sudden shock realized the girl staring back at him was his dear Sarah Ann. He turned the picture over and the back read *Sylvia Marie Patterson 18 yrs old.*

This was not the Sarah Ann he knew. This girl had long auburn hair and skillfully applied makeup. Nothing like the Amish girl he had met and married. His heart beat faster, realizing that in the handwritten pages he may find out more than he had wanted to know about Sarah Ann. For just a moment, he thought of not reading it and throwing it away but knew that he would regret it more later by not knowing than whatever it would reveal.

He slowly unfolded the letter and began to read:

> In the event of her death, Sarah Ann had asked me to pass this on to you. The key is for a storage locker with the name and locker number listed below, by getting her items

from the storage locker you will find the answers to most of your questions.

A Friend of Sarah Ann

Allen slowly lowered the paper to the table. He felt like someone had taken a sledgehammer to his heart and stomach; he could hardly breathe. How was it possible that someone you thought you knew so well would turn out to be someone you didn't know at all? His head spun with thoughts, memories crashing over him. He put his head in his hands and groaned, the grief consuming him.

He sat there for what seemed a long time, but he knew that somehow he had to go on living.

He rose, taking the umbrella back to where it belonged, moving around trying to make sense of his surroundings when all he wanted to do was throw himself on the floor and weep. He made himself a cold meatloaf sandwich using the remainder from the night before. He sat back at the table, chewing it mindlessly, trying to make sense of all he had just read. He opened his satchel, taking out the papers to grade, but after a few attempts and losing concentration he finally gave up and put them back in the satchel to be done later.

He thought of a walk and decided that would eat up time before bedtime while providing a distraction. So he put on his hat, and since the weather was getting cooler, debated on a light jacket, but decided against headed out the door. He'd just walk briskly enough to stay warm.

Allen walked for a long time, making himself notice the scenery, passing by a pond with ducks and staying beside the road as a few cars passed. He wasn't sure of much yet, but one thing he did know, was that whatever was in that storage locker, he had every intention of discovering. Since he had no vehicle himself, he would get on the neighborhood phone to find a ride for the two hour drive as soon as he got back from his walk.

Friday morning dawned with Allen having slept fitfully, the suspense of what lay before him having kept him awake until the wee hours of the morning. He did not feel rested at all, and groaned at having to get up. The school day didn't beckon him nearly as much. All he could think of was living through the day, for Saturday couldn't come soon enough.

He had found a ride to take him to Wooster to the storage unit, but it had taken quite a bit of calling.

For one of the first times in his life, he felt frustration at not having a car of his own as he thought of the convenience and how he could already have gone on his own.

He threw together a sandwich, an apple, the remainder of the pretzels while realizing his lunch was the same as the day before, but not being able to do anything about that until his visit to the store was made. He went out the door and set off for the school, determined to make the best of the day and somehow not let show just how torn up he was on the inside.

Ada Marie was already seated at her desk when he arrived and her cheerful greeting and friendly smile was like a balm to his spirit as he put his hat on the hook and sat at his desk. She wasn't what he considered beautiful but was striking in a very becoming way with her smiling dark eyes, neat brown hair, and full lips. She was one of those who even had she used makeup, would not have needed much, since she had a clear natural skin tone. She was slim, but not to the point of being too thin. He realized that to most men she would be very appealing. But in his grief, she was someone he had no interest in, as Sarah Ann was still so vivid in his mind.

The day progressed much more quickly than he had feared, and before he realized, it was time to dismiss for the day. Shortly afterward, he was walking in the driveway of the Raber's home.

Amos was in the yard, mowing with his push mower. He stopped, resting his arms on the handles as he greeted Allen. "How is school going?" he asked.

"Going better than I had expected and feared,'" Allen replied. "That's good, I am happy to hear that," Amos said with a smile. "We are invited to a hotdog roast tonight, and we were told to bring you along. It's only a half mile, so we can all walk. A few of your students will be there as well." He pulled a handkerchief out of his pocket and wiping his brow. Allen thought this could be a good diversion to a long night at home and told Amos it sounded like fun and he'd go along. He also realized it would also take care of deciding on what to make for dinner. Going into the house, he decided on a nap since he had slept so poorly the night before.

As he lay the satchel down, he realized that grading papers was going to be a never ending task, and sometime over the weekend, he needed to grade the papers he had brought home with him.

Amos had told him they'd leave at six for the hotdog

roast, so he set his alarm for a half hour before.

His eyes closed and he fell asleep nearly as soon as his head hit the pillow.

He woke to the beeping of his alarm clock. Rising, he got up and got himself dressed and ready.

The hour and a half of sleep reviving him, made him feel somewhat better.

As he left to meet Amos and his family for the walk to the hotdog roast, he realized he felt better than any time since reading the letter and living with the trepidation of what he would learn tomorrow.

Chapter 3

Allen sat with the others around the ring of fire, the hot dogs eaten, and S'mores being made. He had tried joining in with the laughter and talking, but he struggled with being able to pay attention to what was being said around him. Unless directly spoken to, he sat in silence.

Looking up, he saw little Anna sitting across the fire looking at him. Smiling at her, he asked "Do you like S'mores"? She nodded, once again ducking her head in a shy manner. "So do I," he said, and just as he finished the sentence, he was handed one. "What good timing," Allen exclaimed, and Anna giggled. The students were more hesitant to approach him away from the familiarity of the classroom. But he could hear many of them running around the yard enjoying the time together. Everyone had been so pleasant to him since his visit that evening and he appreciated the caring he was shown. He had answered lots of questions about his parents, his life at home, and what it was like being an only child. Most Amish had more than just a few children, and being an only child was unusual. Imagining life apart from having many siblings was difficult for them to grasp.

A few also expressed their condolences for his loss. Allen always felt awkward when people expressed sadness for Sarah Ann's death. He knew they only wanted to show they cared, but sometimes it was just easier to avoid talking about it.

The rest of the evening passed pleasantly, and at about half past nine Amos and Saloma gathered the family together for the walk home. "You are welcome to stay longer," his host told him, but Allen replied that he had some things he needed to attend to the next day and had better get his sleep. He thanked them and made his way home. The nap from before had long since worn off, and he longed for the softness of the bed.

He knelt by the bed, trying to gather his thoughts together and quietly cried out to the one he knew could make sense of all of this and somehow help put it all together so it made sense to him and was bearable to carry.

He rose and lay in bed, stilling his troubled mind so it could allow sleep and eventually he drifted off into a deep sleep.

*****

Allen jerked awake, his heart pounding in fright from the dream he felt he had just escaped.

Sarah Ann had been standing over him, looking down at him with a smile on her face, that familiar smile that greeted him when he came home in the evening, true joy at seeing him. He was smiling back and reaching up to touch her face, when suddenly hands had appeared from nowhere, from behind her, grasping her by the shoulders and yanking her back. With a shriek, she was pulled back and out of sight, and he woke, gasping from the reality.

His mouth felt dry so he got up and poured himself some water, drinking deep gulps and draining the glass in a few swallows. He moved to the curtains and pushed them aside, the moonlight shining down and lighting the pasture. He saw the dim shapes of the horses as they grazed, and he briefly wondered when they slept. Letting the curtain fall he moved to the front of the house and looking out the window saw a car slowly passing and thought that a bit odd since the road wasn't a very heavily traveled one. He moved over to the recliner and sat down in the darkness, the silence all around him. Leaning his head back, he closed his eyes and drifted to sleep.

He woke to light coming through the curtains. Looking at the clock, he saw it was half past seven and as he had the driver scheduled for 8:30, he had an hour to get ready.

He took a shower, dressed, and then prepared a bowl of cereal. Reading his devotional book while eating was a daily practice for him, and he and Sarah Ann often had read it together. They would then discuss what they had read. He had liked her open mindedness and the candor in which she saw things, so differently than what he would have had expected, and he now realized a lot of that probably had something to do with how she was brought up, not Amish at all like he had thought. She would often see into matters with a depth that surprised him and with a wisdom he felt a great admiration for. He found himself feeling bitterness rising up within, and he fought against the feeling. He knew bitterness was a root that would only grow into something that could not be good. Taking his empty dish to the sink, he rinsed it out and left it there with the other dishes from the day before. It was only a few minutes before his ride would be there and he didn't want to make him wait.

The tires hummed as they drove along on the freeway. Pat, the driver, talked incessantly, and but for an occasional nod or a yes, Allen really didn't need to contribute much to the conversation. The van was definitely not a very new model, and it shook and made noises, and though Allen didn't know all that much about vehicles, even his untrained ear could tell it was almost ready to sound its death rattle. He had told Pat the name of the storage company when he had arranged the drive and was informed that with a GPS they could find the place very easily. Allen just hoped he was right. He didn't feel like driving all over Wooster and have it seem like he was searching for a needle in a haystack. The GPS device on Pat's cell phone began speaking, informing them to get off at the next exit. His stomach muscles clenched, as Allen realized just how close they were getting.

Pat looked at the phone and said, "Another 3.4 miles is what she's saying we have left."'

The last few miles passed rapidly, as Pat made all the correct turns he was instructed to do, and before long the WE-STOR-4U sign came into sight. Allen told him the locker was C-17, and they pulled up to the gate which was open and drove through and past buildings A and B. They turned right and went down the long row between the B and C building. The C building was backed up against a high block wall. They came to number 17, and Pat stopped. "Here it is," he said. Allen opened his door and got out, pulling his wallet out of his pocket. He had placed the key in there for safekeeping. Pulling the key out of his wallet, he inserted it into the lock that hung on the storage door. It turned, and the lock popped up. He turned the open lock and lifted it off the door. Pulling it open, he peered inside. The room wasn't large, maybe five feet by five feet. There were several large stacking plastic containers and two medium-size cardboard boxes. Pat and Allen grabbed the ends of the containers and together got them loaded. Allen said he'd get the rest and carried the other boxes to the open back doors of the van. They stacked them all inside, and Allen went back, making sure nothing else was laying there that he may have missed. He wondered what to do with the lock and key and thought he'd just leave the unit with them hanging on it with the door unlocked.

The ride home was uneventful, and after refusing Pat's offer for help carrying the boxes into the house and paying the fare, Allen wanted nothing more than to be alone with his thoughts. He was glad no one seemed to be around so he wasn't asked questions about the boxes and containers. He carried the heavy containers inside, his muscles responding to the weight. The years of carrying concrete blocks made the task fairly easy, and he wasn't breathing heavily at all after having carried everything inside. He sat down on his recliner and just looked at them. Now that he had them here it seemed too formidable of a task. He thought of the groceries he needed and decided to go to the store. The boxes could wait. He realized, had he thought of it sooner, he could have asked Pat to take him. But his mind was so much on just getting the items safely into the house that nothing else had mattered.

He wondered if Amos was going to town, and decided

he would go and ask. He knocked on Amos and Saloma's door, and while he waited noticed the dying morning glories that had grown so well and bloomed so beautifully on the trellis on the side of the porch. Allen didn't care for the fall when things died. He much more preferred spring when things came to life. Winter was another season that he would rather have done without. Working outside for so many winters of his life had soured him against liking the cold. He did realize, however, that this year would be different, and for the first time since leaving eighth grade, he would be nice and warm inside for the winter.

The door opened and Amos stood there. Allen smiled and greeted him in Pennsylvania Dutch. "Wie Gehts?"?

Amos smiled back, "Gute," he replied. "I was wondering if you were going to town anytime today" he asked. "Yes, I was going out soon to hitch up. Would you like to ride along?"

Allen said he would.

The horse trotted along, the buggy swaying as it moved along the small grooves worn into the pavement from the wheels of all the buggies having traveled through over the years.

Amos made small talk, and Allen found himself enjoying the visit. He felt comfortable with Amos. He found him to be a man who enjoyed conversation but didn't seem to be putting anyone down in any of the things he said. In a way, he was a bit like Allen's own father who had always reminded Allen of the old adage "If you can't say anything nice about someone, don't say anything at all." Allen had always appreciated his parents and had known them to be very kind to others. He remembered as a child his mother telling him to never mock or make fun of others. She would tell him the story in the Bible of the two she bears that came out and tore up the children who were mocking God's prophet. That story had burned within himself, and he had always made sure to never mock.

They arrived at the grocery store, and as Amos tied up the horse, Allen noticed a car sitting across a few rows of the parking lot with two men sitting inside. It seemed like they were watching him with more interest than was normal, but Allen didn't give it that much thought since the Amish were accustomed to being stared at. He got himself a shopping cart and proceeded down the aisles of the fair sized grocery store. He was pleased at the choices and that they carried his favorite snacks. He finished and got to the checkout before Amos, and after paying for his items he took them out and placed them all in the back of the buggy. He left the curtain unsnapped and got into the front seat, climbing over the wheel. He settled in and waited impatiently for Amos to finish so he could get back home and get started on the boxes. Amos finally arrived at the buggy and Allen jumped back out to help him place his bags inside. They started off and Amos remembered an errand at the hardware for Saloma, so they stopped and Allen opted to wait outside. He saw the old railroad tracks still set up as if waiting for a train that would never come. Amos had told him that the trains had not come through there in over 20 years. Allen thought of his own life and how something within himself seemed just like those tracks, an endless waiting on something he knew would never come. He had never viewed Sarah Ann after her death, her body had been disfigured beyond recognition. He'd been told she had been dragged under the vehicle that struck her down and he had been advised to let his memories be of more pleasant ones and chose not to view her. He had wondered if having seen her somehow would have given him a more sense of closure. But along with so many other things lately, it was just something he had to lay to rest.

Amos climbed in the buggy and they headed for home, the horse picking up the pace now that it sensed it was homeward bound. They turned into the lane and the dog came bounding up to them. Amos refused his offer to help and called his sons over to carry the groceries into the house. Allen gathered all his things together, and glad for the plastic handles of the bags, he was able to carry them all in one single trip. He put all the items away and mentally told himself to remember where he placed them so he wouldn't need to hunt for them later. He got himself a bowl of his favorite snack and went over to his chair. He knew the boxes would be better off in the bedroom in the event anyone coming wouldn't ask. Getting up he moved them to the bedroom, finding space against the wall between the bed and dresser. Placing one of the large containers on the bed, he opened the lid, his breath abated. It held a winter coat laying across other clothes folded neatly in two stacks side by side underneath. He placed the container to the side and looked inside the other container. It, too, was full of clothes. These were more summer, he guessed. He held up a tank top and imagined his Sarah Ann wearing it, knowing that at one time she surely had. He placed it back inside and closed the lid, stacking the container atop the other.

He placed the smallest of the cardboard boxes on the bed, and even before opening the box, he knew that the most important of items were probably inside this one. He lifted the flaps of the closed box and wondered how strange the mind works that he suddenly remembered learning how to close a box in this way from his mother when he was just a young boy.

Inside was a stack of books, old hardcover ones and a few soft covers. Several were classics he himself had read as a child.

There was a nicely lacquered jewelry box, and he lifted it out. Opening the lid, soft, melodious music began to play.

It held several rings, one was a simple gold band and when he looked it over carefully, he noted the inscribed heart on the inside between the letters W.P. M.P. He wondered if the P. stood for Patterson, the last name Sarah Ann had on the back of her photo. He found a heart-shaped locket hanging on a simple gold chain, and opening it saw a smiling couple. They looked to be in their late teens or early twenties. He supposed it was her parents. They looked at the camera with wide open smiles. The picture didn't have the bright crispness of a new photograph but he could still see their expressions clearly. They looked happy, like they had nothing to hide and no fear of the future. He lay the locket aside and digging deeper, he found a key chain with a single key. It was a Disneyland scene, and again, he thought of the two different worlds they had both come from. The box also held several necklaces and different sets of earrings. Allen thought the quality of the jewelry looked good, but he didn't know much about such things.

Allen closed the jewelry box and placed it back inside. He set it on top of the large containers and opened the second box. He found a stack of diaries, a teddy bear, a photo album that had MEMORIES embossed on the cover, and an array of other small mementos from Sarah Ann's life. He pulled out the diaries and journals, finding seven in all. He saw they had dates on the inside and he thought he'd begin with the earliest and work his way to the last. He carried it out to his chair and the snack he had gotten for himself a little while earlier. He settled down and began to read, the words leaping off the pages.

The writing was in a child's hand, seemingly every paragraph had a word or so scratched out with the correction written above. Inside the cover was inscribed Sylvia M. Patterson age 10.

He began to read, losing himself in the pages as he sought to understand Sarah Ann and who she really was.

Chapter 4

"I am not very good at writing. I don't think so, but my teacher has told us that we should begin writing down our feelings on paper because it is a good thing. It allows us to express ourselves and then choose who we want to share them with." Allen smiled as he read the childish writing, written by the hand of a child exactly as it came from the mind.

He continued reading:

I am ten, but I will begin from my earliest memories. So let's say about four. I was in a park, I think. At least it seemed like a park, it was sunny and I was on a swing.....
....

She put her head back, going back and forth on the swing, the sky above them bright blue with a few puffy floating clouds. The sun was bright, shining in her eyes so she could hardly see. She felt her mother pushing her gently on her lower back, slowly pushing her higher and higher. She wasn't afraid and even though she was only four, she knew that no matter how high she was pushed, she'd just want to go higher. "Higher Mommy," she cried as she giggled excitedly. Her mother said, "This is high enough Sylvia, we don't want you falling and hurting yourself."

Eventually, her mother tired of pushing her, and suggested they take a walk around the small lake that held different types of fowl. She saw others feeding the ducks and wished she had bread of her own to share with them. They walked around the water, and as they passed by the swing set and toward the parking lot where the car was parked, she suddenly sensed her mother stiffen.

Having her mother show anxiety was nothing new for Sylvia, but this seemed different somehow, and even her little mind knew that along with the anxiety, there was a real fear. Her mother was looking over her shoulder and she picked up her pace, encouraging Sylvia to walk faster. "I'm trying Mommy, but I can't go any faster," she said. They got to the car and her mother anxiously told her to quickly jump in through the driver's side door and to buckle her seat belt. Her mother didn't bother to fasten her own, but hurriedly rammed the key in the ignition, turned the key and the gravel flew as they quickly drove away. It seemed a long time to Sylvia as her mother sped up streets, turning this way and that and when she finally felt comfortable that she had lost whatever it was she was driving away from, they stopped at a service station and her mother got out of the car and anxiously made a phone call. She knew it was her father, since she heard her mother's frightened voice saying his name several times in her frenzy. Her father must have told her to lower her voice, because she began talking in low tones and Sylvia could no longer make out what she was saying. Sylvia whimpered, "Mommy, I have to go potty." Her mother looked at her, pausing her conversation with her father and said, "Wait a moment, sweetheart, and I'll take you, let me finish my phone call." She hung up the phone shortly after and took Sylvia to the restroom.

When they arrived home, Sylvia was ready for the nap her mother suggested, and fell asleep soon after laying down in her bed. When she woke up several hours later, she was snuggled up in a blanket, laying in the backseat of the car with the seat belt safely buckled around her. Her parents were talking in the front seat. She could barely move her feet, and when she looked, she saw suitcases piled around her, several boxes on the floor. She sat up and her mother noticed she was awake. She turned to her and Sylvia saw the tension on her mother's face. Even at her tender age, she recognized fear, and whatever it was that had her mother so scared, she sensed it from her father as well. That unnerved her, since her father had never shown fear, but always seemed so brave and strong and comforting her mother when she would feel a large amount of anxiety. "Mommy, I'm hungry," Sylvia complained as she felt the hunger pangs. It had been a long while since their picnic in the park and it was just on the verge of darkness now. Malinda handed her a banana, "Here you go sweetheart, this will need to do until we stop in a little while. We want to get as far as we can tonight, and then we'll stop and find a motel and get you a happy meal from McDonald's," her mother promised.

"Where are we going, Daddy?" she asked her father. Will tilted the rear view mirror and smiled back at her, trying to reassure her. "We are going somewhere very nice, where you can have new friends and maybe eventually we can even have a dog or cat. Try and be a big girl, and let's make this a fun time, shall we?" He winked at her in the mirror. Sylvia wasn't too convinced, but she wanted to be a big girl for her father. She loved the times spent with him. Too often, he was gone from her life, working until late at night. She cherished those evenings when he was home to tuck her into bed. He would make the time special by reading her stories and enacting them in funny voices that would make her laugh. And he would always make sure he checked the closet for her, to make sure no scary monsters would come out later and get her while she slept.

Her father turned the radio on and Johnny Cash filled the car, the guitar notes of Walk the Line ringing, as he turned up the sound and began to sing along. Sylvia loved to listen to her daddy sing. The mood in the car lightened as the forced cheerfulness seemed to have a positive effect.

The miles passed and as the radio played her parents continued to sing along.

Her father mentioned the Comfort Inn sign approaching and her mother said it sounded fine.

They got off the next exit and Will pulled into the drive thru of the McDonald's located just off the exit. The promised happy meal was beckoning to Sylvia as her father pulled into the Motel's parking lot. He got out and went inside the office to secure the room. Her mother told her as soon as they were settled in their room she could have her meal.

The next day passed slowly for Sylvia as the long day of driving finally crept to an end.

She saw cows and horses in pastures alongside the moving car, and suddenly her father had to brake as they went over a hill and ahead was a black buggy pulled by a horse. The back of the buggy had a big bright orange triangle shape on the back. They went around the horse and buggy and Sylvia saw little children inside. "Daddy, what is the orange thing on the back of that funny looking thing," Sylvia asked. "It's a triangle," Her father explained, "It is there so cars coming up from behind, like we just did, will know it's a slow moving vehicle and prevent themselves from hitting them." It was the first time Sylvia had seen Amish people before and she was full of questions, amazement at having a horse and buggy instead of a car, and the way the people in the buggy had been dressed. "Will we be living here in the country?" she asked excitedly.

"Well, not exactly in the country perhaps, but in a small town surrounded by the country," her mother told her, turning around to smile at her.

They found a Bed and Breakfast nestled among trees. The proprietors were a Mennonite family who were very welcoming. Although it was after the time that dinner was served, the hosts insisted on serving them leftovers. Mrs. Miller fussed over Sylvia and made sure she chose several homemade cookies from the different choices offered.

Her parents chatted with the Millers and she heard her father asking how far the nearest fair sized town was located and if there would be any places for rent. Sylvia felt safe here and she knew her mother was feeling the same. Malinda seemed more relaxed than Sylvia had seen her in a very long time. Her pretty face was smiling and the worry lines from her brow and between her eyes were gone. Sylvia thought her mother was the most beautiful lady in the world. They had a game they played together, similar to the Mirror, Mirror on the Wall question but her mother had changed the words to reflect a very special rendition of their own. It always made Sylvia happy when they played because it meant her mother wasn't feeling anxiety and was relaxed enough to have fun. The bedroom had a queen sized bed, and their hosts moved a cot in for Sylvia to sleep on. They rose the next morning, greatly refreshed from the comfortable beds, and to a breakfast that must have had Mrs. Miller up very early. Eggs, Sausage and fresh biscuits with honey and homemade apple butter were part of the sumptuous feast. They bowed their heads to pray and Sylvia felt a warm pleasant feeling inside as Mr. Miller blessed the food and she listened to his kind and gentle voice as he asked God to please watch over little Sylvia. Her mother who rarely ate much for breakfast, couldn't stop saying how good the food was and thanking the hosts for their kindness.

Sylvia liked being here in the country, there was a safe secure feeling and she instinctively knew that her parents felt it as well.

Sylvia woke up in her new bedroom, she wasn't sure yet if she cared very much for her room. The home her family was renting came fully furnished but many of the furnishings were rather worn. Her dresser was battle scarred, with marks to prove the test of time spent with countless people not caring how it was treated. It was bright daylight outside and she could hear water running from the bathroom next to her room. Her father was going to be spending his day looking for employment while her mother worked on the finishing touches of get-

getting them settled in.

Her father had asked Sylvia the night before, as he was leaving her room after tucking her in, to please wish him luck. They were making a game out of everything for her, and Will had played a game of what he could do here in their new town. They had gone over all the possibilities, and he had taken the time to explain to her that a doctor could only be a Dr. after many years of studying to be one. That was after she had suggested a doctor, and other things like a fireman or policeman. She got out of bed and went to the kitchen, her mother looked up and smiled when she saw her. Malinda poured her a bowl of cereal and Sylvia was almost done eating when her father came in. He was wearing a suit and tie and Sylvia told him how handsome he looked. The best looking daddy in the world! Will smiled and thanked her, chucking her under the chin as he bent and kissed the top of her head. He kissed Malinda goodbye, picked up his keys and left, the house suddenly seeming very empty and lonely without his presence.

Chapter 5

...**A**llen stopped reading. The room had darkened, and his interest was so deep in the diary that he'd not even realized the time that had slipped by. He set it down and rose to light a lamp.

He thought of church in the morning. Amish went to church every other Sunday. Each church was divided into a small enough group, called districts, making it possible to gather in homes. A tradition that was done many years ago. It gave opportunity to visit neighboring district churches on alternating Sundays, and that was greatly encouraged.

He put together a ham and cheese sandwich with some potato chips, and as he sat at the table to eat, he pondered over what he had just read. Reading about Sarah Ann as a child was interesting, to say the least, but he almost felt he was invading into the life of someone he may really not have known as well as he thought he had. He was tempted to go straight to the end of the stories, to the last book and find if he was in any. But something told him it wouldn't be wise. He needed to be patient, take the time it took to learn to know who Sarah Ann was from the beginning.

He still felt tired but thought now would be a good time to grade the papers so he wouldn't need to leave them for tomorrow. Amish strictly forbade working on Sunday, and he thought the church would probably view grading papers as work, so he would go ahead and get them done. The diary could wait for tomorrow afternoon. Allen spent the remainder of the evening grading papers, and when the last paper was looked over and all appropriate marks were given, he lay his pen down and sighed. His neck was aching, and he rolled it around to loosen the muscles that had bunched from being in the same position so long. He suddenly realized that he hadn't given his clothing any thought for what he was wearing in the morning, and though they were clean, he wasn't sure the shirt still looked ironed. He pulled it out of the closet and thought it looked fine. Sarah Ann always made sure he looked neat, brushing off any loose hair or dandruff from his shoulders.

There were so many things he missed about her, and he remembered all the small ways she made him feel special. How she labored over food, trying her best to make it taste like his mother's. When he had said, just make it like you were taught, she had replied that she never really learned how to cook that well. He had asked why, and she'd kind of evaded the question. Then, he just thought she was shy about not being able to cook, but now, he saw it was more than that. Amish families took pride in passing along age-old recipes, and she was never a part of that kind of tradition.

He rose the next morning before the alarm clock rang, feeling refreshed for the first time in several days. His mind felt clear and he looked forward to church and being with others. It was being held just up the road, easily within walking distance and he wanted to get there with enough time to spare. Being late for church is frowned upon by the Amish, and they are all gathered and ready to worship a healthy amount of time before, most by at least a half hour. He took a shower, shaved and got dressed, putting on his black wool hat. He took one last look in the mirror before leaving. He felt awkward since being widowed. Before being married, he knew where he belonged, and after marrying Sarah Ann, he had been with the young married men. Now he was unsure where he belonged, no longer with the single men but required to be with young married men, who through no fault of their own, gave clear reminders of his loss.

He had wondered why it was called "widowed" when he was a widower and not called widower-ed.

Allen walked down the road, nodding to the passing buggies making their way to the church. He knew that as the new teacher in the area, he was kind of a commodity and just hoped that because of being widowed that no one consider him as a conquest. There was no way he felt ready for that and did not feel up to needing to let anyone know.

He saw Ada Marie outside the washroom entry door, standing with a few other unmarried girls. She gave a slight wave as she acknowledged him, smiling in the friendly way she had each day.

He went on to the barn and walked down the long line of men shaking each of their hands as he went, exchanging greetings. He made small talk until the time came to file into the basement where church was being held.

The hosts heated their hot water with a wood fire held in a contraption that looked like a 50-gallon drum turned on its side with water pipes rising from it. When Allen had seen one for the first time at Amos Rabers house, he had checked it out with a great deal of interest. The church where Allen came from allowed appliances to be operated with propane gas, and the water heater was as well. The fire from the heater had the basement very warm, and Allen felt perspiration gathering sitting among all the warm bodies. The songs were familiar to everyone, and they all sang heartily.

Allen felt warmed by the solemnity of the people as they gave worship to their God.

The sermon was sincere, and he enjoyed listening as the preacher shared several stories from his own life while giving biblical applications to go along with the lessons.

The last song ended and as all the nonmembers filed out, Allen rose with them. Since he was considered a visitor and not a member of this church, he was not required to stay and listen to important matters needing to be discussed.

He went outside and waited for them to come out. Immediately after they were all dismissed, the hosts and other willing helpers placed the benches together forming tables so everyone could be seated for lunch. Allen smeared the homemade bread with mixed peanut butter, along with bologna and Swiss cheese that he had chosen from an array of cheeses that were offered on a large plate. He topped it with dill pickle slices. The sour from the pickles, mixed with the sweetness of the peanut butter, made what he considered a delightful combination. He wondered at the age-old tradition the Amish had put together for a Sunday lunch following church, but it never failed to please and satisfy. He was enjoying listening to the others around him. They all had known each other from birth, and they spent the time together comfortably sharing their week with one another.

He walked home enjoying the weather. The day was nice and sunny, and even though a bit chilly, he didn't mind. He thought of a nap, and then remembered the diary, and debated on which he should do. The diary won, and he took it to the bedroom and lay on the bed and began to read. As he was almost at the end of the first diary, he thought he would finish it before taking a nap.

*****

..........Malinda found a job as well, and she explained to Sylvia that she would be staying with a nice Amish family while her parents were gone during the day. "You remember the nice Miller family," her mother told her as she buttoned her coat to leave. "This family is a lot like them. I think you'll like being there. They have kids too and a little girl about your age. Won't that be fun!" Sylvia didn't know what to think, but she had been told to be brave so many times in her life already, that she didn't fuss as her mother buckled her in the car.

Mrs. Bontrager greeted them at the door. She was plump and her smile lit her whole face. She stooped down and shook Sylvia's hand, telling her how glad she was to meet her. A little girl about her own age, peeked from around her ample skirt. Sylvia smiled shyly at the girl and she smiled back. Mrs. Bontrager pulled her out from behind her and said, "Lena, this is Sylvia who is going to be staying with us during the day while her parents work. It will be up to you to make sure she is happy here." Sylvia already liked Lena. She looked like she'd be fun to play with. Mrs. Bontrager said, "We have puppies in the barn, do you want to see them? Lena, why don't you take Sylvia to the barn and show her the puppies." It was more a command than a question, and Malinda realized she had things she wanted to discuss. The girls scampered off and Mrs. Bontrager poured them both cups of coffee and they sat down at the beautiful oak kitchen table.

Malinda commented at the beauty of the carvings on the sides and chairs, and her hostess replied that, "John bought this for me on our tenth anniversary." She laughed and said, "I know you probably would have chosen a nice piece of jewelry." Malinda smiled and said "Possibly, but I wouldn't have turned down such a lovely table." Her hostess' face became serious and she said, "Now to get to the matter at hand. I am delighted to have your little girl in my home each day, but I'm concerned about the influence it may have upon Lena. If this were for only a day or two, it would be fine but I'm afraid a long term thing may be too much. Will you mind if Sylvia wears Lena's clothes the while she is here?" Malinda knew the threat of keeping the outside world from coming into Amish homes, was a concern for the Amish, and she had wondered about that when someone suggested the Bontragers. She considered for a moment and then said, "No, I think it would be fine. Sylvia will probably think it's a fun adventure." Mrs. Bontrager smiled and said, "It's settled then, you have a place for her to stay." Malinda smiled and thanked her. Relief filling her as she felt the love emanating from the woman. She intuitively knew that Sylvia would be very happy here.

The days that followed were happy ones for Sylvia. She was excited each morning to get up early and have her mother drop her off at the Bontragers. She and Lena would play all day long, mostly dolls, and they took turns acting out stories and playing with the puppies. Mrs. Bontrager always had plenty of homemade cookies and never seemed to mind making them tea for a party.........

*****

Allen set down the book, done with the first of them. He wanted to go on reading and learn what it was that had frightened them so much to the point of fleeing. But his eyelids were heavy, and he thought he'd sit on his recliner and take a nap and continue reading later. So he lay back and dozed off. He began dreaming, and it was a pleasant one.

He and Sarah Ann were sitting on the big swing in his parent's front yard. The swing held two seats facing each other and had a platform which swayed back and forth. They were playing the Five-Letter Word game, and most of the times Allen won. The object of the game was for each player to choose a five-letter word and keep it in their minds while the other player asked you different five letter words and you would tell them how many of the letters were in your secret word. By process of elimination, you would try and see who could be the first to guess the others word correctly. It was a game they both liked to play. Sarah Ann gave the word flake, and he laughed and asked if it had a double meaning. She was laughing, as he woke from the dream. He just lay there, willing it to continue. The dream was so different than the last one he had of her. This one was so typical of their life together. Because of the joy he knew their love carried, there had to be a valid reason that kept her from telling him everything about herself.

Chapter 6

He got out of bed and went to the kitchen, feeling hunger building since the lunch he had at church.

He got out some ground beef and made himself a cheeseburger. He missed the salads his mom and Sarah Ann had made. He liked eating healthy foods and thought his body must be in shock with all the snack foods it had been fed lately. He ate slowly, munching his way through the burger and chips and washing it down with water. He decided that sometime in the future he'd like to pursue more about the Bontrager's. It had not been mentioned exactly which town they lived in, and he knew that looking for an Amish family with a common name in the Holmes County area in Ohio would be like looking for a needle in a haystack kind of thing. He rose and thought that he'd go for a walk. Since he wasn't doing the difficult labor anymore, he was concerned with the possibility of gaining weight and wanted to do all he could to prevent that from happening. Walking also helped him keep a clear head. Lots of times throughout his life, he had managed to solve many of his problems and issues that arose by taking a good walk.

Amos had told him before that he was welcome to walk in the woods. The neighbors that bordered the back property and owned all the land going back at least a mile, had given permission for them to walk on their property as well. Allen thought it would be a nice place to take a hike, and he figured he had about a good hour of daylight left. He put on a warm jacket, some boots in case he'd encounter some muck, and went for his walk.

He wasn't much of a hunter, but he enjoyed looking at the deer tracks and other tracks he guessed were of a fox. He startled some quail and watched as they flew off with a whir of wings. Nature was so beautiful to Allen. It was a balm to his soul and a closeness he would feel to his maker being surrounded by His creation. The leaves were beginning to change colors and he admired the different shades.

He returned from his walk and was looking forward to getting into the second diary when Daniel, one of Amos and Saloma's sons came and asked if he'd like to come over for the evening. They were going to play Pictionary and thought he may like joining them. Daniel was a nice and polite student who was in the sixth grade. Allen appreciated Amos and Saloma's children. They were all very polite and respectful. Allen told Daniel to tell his parents that he'd be over in a little while. He thought the reading could wait and found himself wanting to play a game and be with people again.

Allen had always found that being an only child made it very easy for him to fade into the background. Being alone was a common thing, and one he felt safe with. But being with Sarah Ann and her friendliness with others, he had been made to step out of that and learned to enjoy being with others more. He saw the healthiness of it, and knew that he would need to put forth an effort to prevent himself from sliding back into the old way of letting life go by while he spent it by himself. He went over to Amos's house and enjoyed the evening playing with their family. It was a very enjoyable time, and Saloma served coffee and several choices of pies. So much for my walk, he thought, as he ate the pie. He knew that others would scoff if they knew his thoughts, but he just wanted to be careful. Becoming overweight doesn't just happen overnight, so there had to be something good in taking precautions.

He thanked them for their hospitality and went back home. Lighting the lamp, he pondered whether he should read some or go to bed. He decided he'd get his lunch ready for school the next day and then got himself ready for bed, being sure to include in his prayers that he not have any haunting dreams.

The week passed without much event. The school days flowed together as Allen and Ada Marie slowly got into the routine of things. The children were responding well to Allen's guidance, and he had wondered why the school had a reputation as they all seemed to listen and behave for him. Amos said it had a lot to do with a person's consistency, and he thought Allen was a good choice for the school. Those few words made him feel very nice, because he knew Amos spoke them from a sincere heart. Allen had read through the next diary and not really found that much more about Sarah Ann that would help him, as she continued playing with Lena and she was slowly learning the language of the Amish people. After the children were dismissed on Friday afternoon, he realized that no matter what he found out about Sarah Ann, nothing would be bringing her back into his life again.

Any amount of closure he may think he would feel wouldn't make up for the loss. Was it better to just let it go, continue on with his life and somehow let time mend his broken heart? On his walk home, he thought how they had met. The memory so real, as if it were yesterday. His church youth group had been invited to spend a Saturday with another small settlement that was located about 50 miles from where he and his family lived. He had gone with no intention of meeting anyone. He had met all the available girls and none had ever given him any romantic notion before. But this time turned out to be different.

Allen was playing the position of first baseman and Sarah Ann had just hit the ball, a grounder that went right over third baseline for a base hit. She was standing on the base, and he couldn't help noticing her beauty. Her hair was a light auburn and she had, what she later told him, were hazel eyes. He was actually so struck by her, that he just stood there, completely aware of her, but unable to speak. She spoke suddenly, "Du zilscht mich net griah. You are not going to get me."

He laughed, "Miah sehna mohl vaeha sell. We will see about that'" He grinned back. Just then the ball flew through the air and landed deep in center field, the catcher not making it there in time.

Sarah Ann ran to second base and stood there smiling back at him triumphantly, and he knew she was right. He had not gotten her. It wasn't until much later that night, as he lay in bed smiling to himself, remembering the beautiful girl who had caught his eye and heart, that he wondered if she had intended what she said to have a double meaning. He didn't forget about her, and several weeks later he hinted around and found the address of the place where she was staying and wrote her, asking if he could come see her. He was delighted when she replied back, that yes, he could. But, she added, please don't expect this to go anywhere. I really am not looking for anyone. That kind of dampened his spirits a bit, but nonetheless Allen couldn't forget how she had made him feel, and he had to at least try.

The walk home ended and stopped his reverie. He arrived at his door and noticed the large manila envelope laying against the wall next to the door. He picked it up as he went inside and saw it was from his mother. She was forwarding all of the mail he'd received since he had been gone. Along with a bank statement and a few bills, he was happy to see several of his favorite magazines. He opened the accompanying letter from his mother and read the latest news of what was happening with his father and the community. He smiled as she related the news of twin boys to a neighboring Amish family who already had six girls and the father had despaired of ever having a son. She finished by saying that his father had decided to take this opportunity of Allen leaving, to slow down and not work so hard. They were looking into opening a small business of their own. Allen was glad to hear that. His father had always believed in hard work and as he had gotten older Allen could often see that the days were tiring him out, but he knew that getting his father to admit it would be another story. He sat down and got involved in one of the magazines for a while until it was time to prepare dinner. After he had cleaned up the dishes, he settled down with a cup of coffee and started in on the next diary.

*****

..........I am nine years old today, and I reminded my dad that someday I'd really like a pet. But he still hasn't promised when. I know my parents are afraid of something and I don't know what it is. One time I was asking my mom about it because I remembered how scared she was in the park that day. But she told me that it was something we can't talk about. That as I grew older I'd learn that there are certain things in life we are all better off never knowing. That confuses me because I don't like that they are keeping a secret from me like that. I can feel it is something very big because I will never forget how afraid my mom was, and even my dad was afraid. But I like it here in this little town. Living in the country is fun and I love Lena more than anyone else in the whole world, next to my parents. I can't wait for Sunday. My parents are going to be gone over Sunday and have asked the Bontragers if I may stay with them. Mrs. Bontrager said that if my parents approved of me going with them to church, I may stay. Mommy and Daddy said they don't mind, so I am spending a night over. I have never spent the night there and I am so excited!

Mrs. Bontrager woke the girls Sunday morning and they both dressed for church. Sylvia had never worn the white organdy apron front that went over the top of the dress before and she felt very dressed up wearing it. It was starched to the point of almost being able to stand on its own.

She was told to be careful so it wouldn't get to looking "runzlich," wrinkled. She had been on many buggy rides since meeting the Bontragers over four and a half years.

Sylvia loved riding in the buggy and had settled well into their home. Her grasp of the Pennsylvania Dutch language had gotten so good that people exclaimed when they realized she was not Amish.

They got to the church, and when she and Lena were surrounded by the other girls, she was suddenly shy. Being with Lena was one thing, but suddenly being around a half dozen was a totally different thing altogether. The girls were all very welcoming, and it didn't take long for her to lose her shyness.

They got seated in the rows of ladies beside Mrs. Bontrager and waited for the men to come in. She asked Lena why the men didn't sit with the women and Lena said she didn't know, but that was how it had been as long as she remembered and had never thought of it before. The men filed in and soon they were all singing a song that she thought sounded very sad. It was in a language she didn't understand and she didn't care very much for the singing. The song finally ended and a little while later a bowl was passed around with a few kinds of cookies and pretzels. Lena leaned over and whispered that it was just for the little kids and they were too old. Sylvia was disappointed. She thought it looked good and had looked forward to having some. The first preacher she didn't care for as much. She thought he looked too stern, and as his voice rose and fell, she was glad when he finally got to the end. They knelt to pray, and then the second preacher started on a sermon. She wondered how long the church service lasted. It wasn't turning out to be as much fun as she thought it would be and the hard wooden bench was becoming very uncomfortable. The preacher started relating a story and she suddenly was interested. He spoke about a time in his life that had happened when he was a child. One that had frightened him very badly. He then specifically spoke to the children and admonished them if they were ever fearful, that God cared, and they could always turn to Him, because they would never get turned away. He spoke with so much caring, such conviction, that Sylvia was struck by it, and she wondered if her mother believed that as well. Her parents believed in God, but they had only taken her to church a handful of times. She had gone to Vacation bible school several times in her life and had enjoyed learning about Jesus. Church finally ended. She and Lena played outside with the other girls until they were called in to eat, where they again, sat with Mrs. Bontrager around the table with all the other ladies and girls.

Her parents picked her up late that afternoon and asked how she had liked going to church.

She said it was fine, but wasn't sure that she'd care to go again.

Sylvia was in fourth grade now and things were going well. She had made some friends at school, but would always consider Lena her best friend of all. The school bus dropped her off at Lena's home each afternoon and she spent several hours there until her mother picked her up later when the time came to get off from work. Her father worked as a car salesman driving all the way to

Akron each day. Several nights a week, he worked late, not arriving home until after Sylvia was already in bed. She didn't care for that very much, since it meant she didn't get to see him as much as she liked. Malinda was working in a bank in a neighboring town. She was an assistant to the branch manager and was, without being told, her employer's right hand. She was very efficient and performed her job well.

It is my tenth birthday today and I got a new diary. I also got the new Celine Dion CD. My friends can't understand why I like her so much, but I think she has the most beautiful voice in the world. I also got some clothes but I'm not too sure if I like the tee shirt. My mom doesn't seem to get it that I'm getting too big for kid's stuff. But I'll wear it anyway. At least once so I won't hurt her feelings.

It's beginning to feel kind of weird wearing the Amish clothes, but I know that is the only way I can keep going to the Bontrager's and I'll do that rather than not be able to be with Lena.

We agreed yesterday that no matter what happens in life, even when we are old and gray, that we will be able to count on each other. I tried to do the pinky swear, but she said the Amish don't swear like that, but she was allowed to promise. So we promised to be best friends forever.........

Chapter 7

. . . I am writing this from the backseat of the car. I think we are once again running from something. This same thing happened before when I was four and I remember a little bit of it. When I asked, my parents said that my dad has a job offer in Phoenix, Arizona and we need to leave now to get there in time. I want to believe them, but I am not sure that I can and not sure what that even means. I asked my mom if I will ever see Lena again, and she said that she hopes so. I don't know what that means either. We are driving on a freeway and my mom is suggesting the ABC license plates game. We are in the motel now. It's not the nicest motel, but at least the TV has some good channels. We had pizza for dinner and my dad was trying to make me feel happier, but I can't help myself. I already miss Lena and since the Amish don't have a telephone, I won't ever be able to call her. I hope Phoenix is as much fun as they are trying to convince me it will be. We had breakfast at Denny's. It was okay, but now I'm feeling kind of carsick. Mom told me to put my head near the open window and breathe in the fresh air. I'm trying to be happy for my parents' sake, but it's not easy when I'm not feeling well, and I'm also very disappointed that a fun summer with Lena will not be happening. We are in Oklahoma now and dad said we'll be in Texas soon. I want to see Texas. Last year I had to write a book report on someone famous and I chose Barbara Bush. I don't know why I picked her. My friends all picked actresses and singers. I think one reason was because I wondered why she always wore such a boring necklace. I found out she just wore it to hide a wrinkled neck. That was really weird, and then I thought, for her to admit it was even more weird and even kind of cool.

Texas is nothing like I thought it would be. It's flat and boring and smells like cows. I can't wait to get through it and be in New Mexico.........

*****

They arrived in Phoenix late the next day, and Will found a Super 8 right off the freeway. Malinda took Sylvia to Kmart to find some things they hadn't remembered to get in their rush to leave. They got back to the motel, and Malinda stopped at the desk to ask for a newspaper. Sylvia wondered why she needed a newspaper, and her mom replied that it was to find an apartment. Her father was gone when she woke, and she assumed he was at his new job.

Her mother finally found a furnished apartment for them that day. Sylvia had grown tired of the search, as they had gotten lost twice, and stopped at numerous gas stations for directions. Each place tried explaining to them that Phoenix was laid out like a grid and all the streets went either north and south or east and west, but it seemed like Malinda still managed to get lost. They arrived back at the motel exhausted, and when Will came home, they all went out for dinner. Will teased Malinda about getting lost and then explained to her how the city had the streets on the east side and the avenues were all on the west side.

They moved in the next day with the little they had. The furniture in the apartment was nice, and Sylvia thought the place even smelled nice. Her mother said the extra they were paying in rent was worth it for the neighborhood and the cleanliness of the complex.

*****

..........Allen stopped reading as he remembered a conversation with Sarah Ann. He had told her that lots of Amish people go to Phoenix to spend winters, and she had said, yes, she'd seen them there. Asking what she meant by that, Sarah Ann replied that she'd been there one winter.

He recognized that so many more hints had been dropped but he had just been so willing to not see. He saw the willful blindness on his part to choose to not see what was now so obvious. That there had been so much more to Sarah Ann than he had ever wanted to look into because he had been too afraid of the truth and thought not knowing was a better thing.

The next day was Saturday and Allen realized it was time to clean the house. It was something he had never had to do much of, but knew that he'd better not let it get out of hand. He lay the diary aside on the stand next to the chair. He wanted to get a letter sent off to his parents as well, thanking them for forwarding his mail and let them know how things were going with school. His mother had asked and he wanted to ease her fears that all was going well. He decided to do that right away, so it would be out of the way and he got a pen and paper and began to write. He told them amusing little stories about a few of the students and how one in particular seemed to always be finding himself in trouble, seemingly through no fault of his own.

Allen ended the letter with a postscript asking his mother if Sarah Ann had ever mentioned knowing a Bontrager family from Ohio. Knowing by asking that he would need to come up with a suitable answer if she wanted to know why he had inquired.

Allen remembered that he needed a few things from the store again, it had been almost a week since being there with Amos. He had seen one of Amos' sons riding a bike with a large basket on the front. He would ask Amos in the morning if it would be possible to borrow the bike since he didn't mind the three-mile ride to the store and wouldn't be getting more things than the basket would hold.

The bicycle tires whirred as he pedaled to the store the next morning. He had slept in an hour later than he normally did, gotten out of bed and had made himself clean the house. He had dusted the house and swept the floor, shaking off the hand loomed rugs and had found a mop and bucket in the washroom. He mopped the floor, and when it was dry had placed the rugs back where they belonged. He looked over everything he had done and felt pleased with his efforts.

As he pedaled along, he thought back with longing how he loved to sit next to Sarah Ann and just touch her, of how one time he was pulling on her ear lobe and noticed a small hole. Looking at the other one he had commented that it, too, was the same. She had stammered a little and said that her ears had always looked like they were pierced, and she'd probably been born that way.

The Amish strictly forbid the wearing of any jewelry; even a wedding ring was out of the question. Allen knew that whatever it was that had kept Sarah Ann from sharing the truth about herself, and maybe even had taken the life from her, must have been something very serious. He realized that reading the journals so far only made him miss her more. She would never have lied to him without knowing that whatever she shared would only endanger his own life, and though he hated the lying with everything within him, he found it easier to not be angry at her knowing the danger she had been in.

He got to the store and parked the bicycle outside in the bike rack. The automatic doors opened to let him through, and he chose a basket and went to gather the needed items. He arrived home, the bike ride had invigorated him, and he was looking forward to the evening with a few of the Amish bachelors in the area who had invited him to get together to play Rook. It was a card game he had always enjoyed and was good at. Playing it as a four-player partner game was what he found the most fun, and they had needed the fourth player, so he was happy to sit in. In church, he had met the host, who had invited him saying several others would be there as well. The prospect of spending the evening with his peers after a long week spent with children was appealing. He had several hours before leaving for his card game so he thought he'd pick up where he'd left off reading the night before.

*****

.........Wow, the summer has been hot here in Phoenix. I am liking my school and my teacher is nice. She asked where I was from and I told her from Ohio. My parent's sat down with me after we got to Phoenix and said if anyone ever asked we were from Ohio but never to mention that I ever lived in Florida. I asked them why and they said when I was older they would tell me, but for now just do as they say. I know now for sure that there is a lot more that they aren't telling me but I guess I won't know until I'm older.

I am invited to Amy's house for a birthday party. She said her mom wanted her to invite up to six girls but she wasn't sure who to invite because she doesn't have that many friends. She just moved to Phoenix too just like me and I am excited to go. Amy is kind of chubby and already I've seen people making fun of her and that makes me mad. Anyway, I'm going with my mom later to get her a gift and I thought today that even though she is chubby and Lena is thin, so she reminds me a lot of Lena. She is nice to everybody even the ones who make fun of her.

The party was fun and I made more friends, but I still miss Lena. I hope she remembers our promise. I just wish she had been allowed to do the pinky swear.

I am fourteen today, sorry diary but I have neglected you. I picked you up several times but didn't have much to say so I didn't.

I'm going to the movies tonight with a guy named Richie. My mom and dad weren't too happy about it but since Amy is going along they said it was okay. I was right about Amy, she is like Lena. I still miss Lena and think about her all the time. I think friendships made when you're kids are the ones that will last the longest but that's just what I think. Anyway, back to Richie, he's really cute and I know a lot of other girls are jealous of me. I know, you're thinking Richie Rich and he hates that too. The movie totally made his name a nightmare, he has to hear about that all the time. I'm glad my name isn't something dumb like that.

My parents took me to the London Bridge today, Amy was allowed to go along. It was really cool seeing the bridge that was actually from the song I learned as a kid. It's in Lake Havasu City and I was kind of freaked out hearing about how some people believe the soul of Jack the Ripper was transported to the United States by one of the bricks of the bridge. I wondered who would be dumb enough to believe that but I guess at least enough do that makes a story like that seem true.

My dad said that's just like the Brits, looking for any excuse to dump their embarrassments on us and my mom told him he's being silly. No idea what he just said but that's my dad.

I am a sophomore! It was a lot different walking in this year than last year and I know much more what to expect. I like high school a lot and Amy and I are in a lot of the same classes so that's very cool.

I haven't told my parents but I wrote Lena a letter. I went online in the school library and searched for their name and address. I didn't remember the road, but I know the town and state and so I'm pretty sure I have the right address. I am excited to see if she writes back, but when she does my mom will find out since she almost always gets the mail. I don't care though because having them find out is a risk I'm willing to take. I miss Lena so much and I just hope she misses me at least half as much as I do her. I have so much to tell her but I didn't want to say too much in case that wasn't the correct address. I'll catch her up with my life when she gets back to me.

I like school well enough but I'm having difficulty with algebra, but I'm not the only one so that makes me glad. Amy is a whiz at it, and she's been helping me but I just can't seem to get the hang of it.

I asked my mom tonight if we can have a talk soon because I have lots of questions for them; she told me we will. She said "My-my, you sound serious," and I told her that it was serious. When a kid grows up without grandparents, no aunts or uncles or cousins, wouldn't you wonder? I also told her that she and dad had better come up with some good answers because I wasn't going to buy their explanations anymore. She got this real funny look on her face and I felt sad for just a little bit and actually thought of letting it go, but I can't. It's my life, and I have a right to know about my life, right? I am really bugged right now and I can't tell anyone, I love Amy, but she's not Leah and something holds me back from telling her. My mom wants me to sign up for choir and maybe I will, that or learn an instrument and be in the marching band.

In a few minutes Friends will be on, I love that show. It's a half hour that I can forget my problems and pretend to be someone else. I love Jennifer Aniston and I want to be just like her.

I got a letter from Lena today!!! I was so excited when I got it and my mom was actually not the one to get the mail, I was which was weird because she's always made it clear that she wants to get it first. Luckily, Mom wasn't home and it's been over a week and I knew the letter would be coming any day if Lena had gotten mine. And guess what??? She misses me just as much as I've missed her. Now I am going to write her back and tell her everything. I feel like something has been placed back inside my body that was removed. That's probably weird to say but it's like an empty spot was now filled and I have it back.

She told me her Mom said hello and would love to see me again and that she'll send me some cookies in the future. My mouth waters remembering her delicious cookies........

*****

Allen lay the book aside and thought of the photo album he had never opened. It was something he hadn't wanted to see before. The realization of a whole other person represented in pictures was something he had feared would just be too hurtful. He had never bothered to see even though the temptation had been there. He thought now would be a good time, and he went to the bedroom to the box he knew it to be in. Taking out the big brown photo album with MEMORIES embossed on the front, he returned to the living room placing it on his lap. Slowly he opened it and saw photos of a little girl with her parents, they looked happy in the poses. Even as a little girl he could see the grown up Sarah Ann. Her beautiful eyes looking shyly at the camera. He flipped through each page, seeing the transformation of her growth in each page. He saw the one where she was fifteen and SOPHOMORE was written at the top of the page and knew that was her age now in the part where he was reading in the diary. Allen thought suddenly that if he went on in the album he may end up seeing photos he may not wish to see. And though he was brought up in an Amish home and attended their parochial school, he still knew about the proms and dances that public schools held. He just may see her in a photo with someone else. He knew that was something his heart couldn't bear to see, and he decided to read more of the diary first and then catch up in the album as time progressed.

Chapter 8

He wondered about Lena and knew that soon he was going to try and find her. It surely wouldn't be that difficult; he had her name and there couldn't be that many Lena Bontragers in that part of Ohio. Noticing it was almost time to leave to spend the evening with his new friends, Allen returned the diary and photo album to the bedroom. He placed them on the nightstand in case he felt like reading more later when he returned.

Monday morning came, and he woke up with a headache. His last few days had been so engrossed in reading and focusing on what he was learning that it was almost more than his mind could absorb.

He dressed and got ready for the day, making himself oatmeal and a cup of coffee. "Maybe the caffeine will help my headache," he thought. The house had a chill, and he knew he'd soon be needing a fire in the stove and would fill the wood box when he got home later that evening. His night with the guys had gone alright, but he had felt a certain emptiness while with them. He wondered what they would have said had he told them of the turmoil his life was in right now.

He felt the same way Sylvia had described in her diary, that someone had removed something from within him, leaving a huge, empty void. He gathered a few things together for his lunch and picking up his satchel, put on his hat and left for school. Since it had rained during the night, the dirt road was full of night crawlers that lay stretched out on the wet road. He remembered how in school he had learned about earthworms and that in rich soil each acre could have up to 1,750,000 worms, and the weight of them under the ground could be more than the weight of livestock living upon the land. Then that had seemed unbelievable to him, but he supposed anything was possible. Just like not knowing what was underground could be the same as not knowing what people hid in their lives. He had found that out firsthand and thought of things about himself he would never feel comfortable sharing with others.

He arrived at school and after hanging his hat on the hook decided a small fire in the wood stove would take the chill from the air before the children arrived. He quickly got one started, thankful for the thoughtful preparation someone had made.

Ada Marie arrived just as he closed the stove door and thanked him saying, "That is going to be a regular thing soon."

Allen agreed and seating himself at his desk took out the papers he had graded and set them on the edge of the desk to give to each student later.

He made small talk with Ada Marie, discussing the weekend, and wondered why he hadn't just fallen for someone like her. But Allen knew that he had met many girls just like Ada Marie and none had sparked an interest in him. They had lacked something, and when he had met Sarah Ann it was the first time that he had known what it was to feel really attracted to someone. His attraction to her had hit him like a brick and she had been all that had been on his mind since. Even in death, her hold over him hadn't loosened, and he pondered if somehow that had to stop. It was a consuming grip that he had to actively break free of, but Allen didn't know if he knew how. His headache had somewhat subsided, and he was grateful for that, because headache or not, the school performed on a schedule and the singing would not have helped his pain. Time for classes came, and he spent the day trying his best to put his heart into teaching, but it wasn't easy, and he was glad when the day finally came to an end.

The earthworms had all but disappeared when he left for his walk home, and he knew either they had gone back into the ground or the hungry birds had seen an easy meal.

Allen missed his parents; being away from them was more difficult than he had thought it would be. He had never been away from his parents for longer than a week before this point; now it had been three weeks, and homesickness was beginning to set in. After his supper after he had filled the wood box when Amos met him while on his way in from the barn. They chatted for a while and Allen contemplated sharing with Amos what was going on in his life. He instinctively felt that Amos would be trustworthy and keep what he was told in confidence. Allen decided to wait but thought maybe in the future he may share with Amos and seek his counsel. He washed his hands and sat down to read

*****

.......Will told Sylvia they would have their talk after dinner that evening. Anxious to have this talk, dinner had dragged on for Sylvia. Her parents were trying to seem normal, but she could tell they were uncomfortable. They made small talk, asking about her day. Sylvia put the dishes in the dishwasher, and after the table was wiped down and leftovers placed in the refrigerator, she and her mother headed into the living room where her father was waiting. Malinda sat on the sofa, and Will got up from his chair to join her. Sylvia sat down in the only other chair. Now that the time had finally arrived she was suddenly shy and felt like she wanted to bolt from the room.

Will explained they had wanted to keep things from her to spare her from any pain and allow her to have a normal childhood. They had never told her but now they believed she was old enough to know.

Malinda and Will were both in the foster care system and lost contact with all family. The reason they were on the run was because there was a misunderstanding when Will was young. He left a foster home after hitting the man over the head with a bottle when the foster parent wouldn't stop beating another child. Will was 17 and ran after finding out the man had died, never wanting the law to find him. They met at a community college where they were both taking classes, fell in love, and got married. Sylvia came along a year later.

They continued to tell her that the day they were in the park, Malinda had thought she was being followed. Even though she may have been mistaken, they didn't want to take any chances of being discovered and therefore rushed off to Ohio.

Sylvia was a little freaked out learning her father had hit a man over the head with a bottle hard enough to kill him, but she did believe him when he said it was for a good reason. She was saddened that her parents had lived such sad lives and asked them a few more questions. She didn't get much satisfaction from her questions so she dropped it, grateful to have found out what she had.

At least now, she no longer felt so uprooted. She had answers for what had been gnawing at her for the past five years.

Her life went on for a while, uninterrupted, and the school days passed. She learned algebra; it was like a light bulb went off in her head one day, and the formulas all began making sense. She thought it was a lot like her life and wrote of it as the biggest metaphor she had ever encountered.

Prom came along, and she went with a date. Allen saw the photo in the album, and it hadn't bothered him like he'd thought it would. Sylvia was now choosing her college, and that took up much of her time. Her grades weren't high enough to grant her a full scholarship, but they were high enough to get her into most colleges of her choice and she really didn't want to go far from home. She considered Grand Canyon University and settled on University of Arizona. She chose sociology, and since Tucson was only an hour and a half away from her parents, considered it to be the perfect option, as it allowed her to be with them on the weekends. She needed to get her driver's license before she left home in six months, she had never concerned herself about it that much. School was within walking distance, and her mother was always willing to take her where she needed to go. She also knew adding her on the insurance would raise the premium, and she didn't want her parents to feel that added burden since they were already paying most of the tuition for college. She had continued her friendship with Lena, and Sylvia's parents had requested that she do it through telephone. Lena walked to her neighborhood phone each week and they would talk for a long time. Sometimes, they'd need to stop so others could use the phone since it was shared by more than a dozen families. But then she'd call back, and they'd go on as if uninterrupted.

Sylvia treasured the phone calls, and they never lacked for things to talk about. She found herself missing the simple life she had experienced over the years spent at the Bontragers. She had often even fantasized about someday leaving her life for one with the Amish but knew that wasn't very likely. They were both nearly eighteen now, and although both liked boys and enough mention was made of them in their conversations, neither one had a serious interest in anyone.......

*****

Allen understood now how Sarah Ann had seemed so content living a quiet Amish life. Although he himself never knew anything different, he didn't think it was anything he'd want to exchange for something else. He had one diary left and a journal and then he would have them all read. He hadn't found anything significant yet but had liked reading about Sarah Ann growing up as a young Sylvia. He opened the diary and began to read:

I have one more week at home and then I leave for college, life is going to be so different but I'm ready. Amy will be going to Northern Arizona University and although she will be a little farther away, she intends on coming home to her family one weekend a month so we'll still get to see one another. We are having a sleepover at her house on Friday evening, one last fun fling before we leave. We've been on a Kellie Martin kick and we are determined to watch everything she's been in. We started with the Christie Series and then we saw Troop Beverly Hills and next it will be The Face on the Milk Carton.

*****

..........Sylvia was in disbelief. What she had just found was staggering to her and the simple curiosity that had prompted her to look for something innocent had just turned into something larger than life itself. Her parents were gone for several hours and she had the house to herself. She had just seen "The Face on the Milk Carton" movie starring Kellie Martin. She had felt herself drawn to the film like there was a shared kinship to the character who discovered that she was kidnapped from her real family and raised by strangers for the past 13 years.

She had never seen her birth certificate before and wondered if she looked for it if perhaps she could find it among her parent's things. She felt a certain amount of guilt for snooping, but curiosity won and she decided to search. And search she did. She began with her mother's things, going through each drawer, and then she carefully moved all the items in her father's dresser drawers. Making sure not to move anything she wasn't immediately touching so she could quickly dash from the room if they suddenly returned. She found a key in her father's sock drawer, pushed all the way to the back corner. It was on a small simple ring and she looked around for what it could go into. Moving a few suitcases in the closet, she found a small safe and when she tried the key, found that it readily opened. Inside were lots of papers, several computer discs and some coins and mementos, her parent's birth certificates, an old driver's license, marriage certificate and as she looked through the envelopes, found an official looking one with a return address of Florida Department of Health. Opening it, she found a birth certificate for a baby born as Julia Elaine Hudson. In disbelief she saw that whoever the baby was they shared the same birth date. Was this her sister she wondered? Looking at the name of the birth mother, she saw it was not her mother and neither was her father mentioned on the paper.

Her heart pounding, she put the papers back in the safe trying to arrange them like she'd found them.

Returning the key to the sock drawer, she looked around the room making sure it was how she had found it. She wondered how she was going to possibly greet her parents like nothing had happened.

She realized what she found helped explain what she had always felt and knew now that whatever her parents told her, she would not believe them. Whatever danger they were in connected directly to her, and like the movie she wondered if they really were actually her parents. What had started off as a fun evening with Amy – a sleepover and a movie – had now turned into a nightmare.

She had one more week before she left and while at college she'd try to find out on her own what it was that Will and Malinda had kept hidden from her all these years. What lies had they covered up and why?

She decided to keep quiet about her find and go on as best as she could pretending everything was fine. If they could do it for eighteen years, she could do it for a week and she also knew she would not be coming home as often on the weekends as originally planned. She'd find something to tell her parents when that time came. She supposed if she really was their daughter, then making up logical stories shouldn't be an issue for her since they had done so well. Hopefully, she thought ironically, that was something she'd inherited from them."

Sylvia settled in at University of Arizona and liked her dorm mate. She was a bubbly girl from Idaho named Kaitlyn who said that Tucson was the largest city she had ever seen. Kaitlyn and Sylvia looked enough alike to be sisters, and even their hairstyles were the same, and it wasn't long before they both became fast friends. She was excited to see Phoenix, and Sylvia promised that she could sometime go along to visit her parents. She settled in to her classes, and life seemed to take on a routine.

Sylvia had no luck finding anything in her online search for the name on the birth certificate. She tried everything she could think of for the state of Florida in her searches and though it revealed suggestions close to what she sought, nothing matched exactly.

She shelved the search, and although she dreaded more than ever knew that another talk with her parents was going to need to happen. She wouldn't be the gullible girl who had so readily believed everything before but this time would demand answers and not stop until she felt within herself that they had told her all. It had been three weeks now since she'd left home and her mother was going to be picking her up for the weekend. Kaitlyn had asked if she was able to go along, and Sylvia didn't have the heart to refuse. She had planned on having a serious talk with her parents but hoped that could still take place. Malinda picked them up early Friday afternoon, luckily for them they had no later classes and were free to leave. Amy was home, too, for the weekend and they had plans the next day for the three to go to the mall together.

She and Kaitlyn had settled in her room, and she had called Amy to make sure the plans for the next day were still in effect. Will and Malinda both seemed to like Kaitlyn, and the conversation flowed easily around the dinner table.

They arrived home, and Kaitlyn said she'd like to take a shower and they could watch the movie later. Sylvia remembered the movie that Amy had offered to her earlier, and she asked Kaitlyn if it would be okay if she'd go and pick up the movie while she was taking a shower. Kaitlyn agreed that it was fine, and Sylvia told her that she'd be back soon and left, walking the short distance to Amy's house. They had missed each other and had lots to share and before she realized it had been gone from home for 45 minutes. She told Amy she had to get home to Kaitlyn and left with the movie.

She arrived home, hearing the television in the living room. She went in to the living room to let her parents know she was home and stopped in shock and disbelief. Horror rising up in her as she saw her parents, both lying in pools of blood, each had a bullet hole in the middle of their foreheads. Malinda was lying on her left side with her hand stretched out and her right lying against her chest like it lay where it had fallen from trying to shield herself. Will was in the recliner, lying back with his head to the side and his chin tilted down a little. She could tell they were both dead, their eyes lifeless. She moaned, clutching her throat as she sucked in her grief, pain setting in dully as the horrifying reality took over. She remembered Kaitlyn and went upstairs, never thinking that whoever had killed her parents could still be in the house. She found her lying just inside the bathroom door, her hair still half damp from her shower, her clean pajamas top had sprinkles of blood on the front that looked like it had splattered in a design. She, too, had a bullet hole in her forehead.

Sylvia went to the phone and called 911, telling them in heaving sobs what she had found. The 911 dispatcher had to ask her several times to repeat herself and when asked if the intruders were still in the house, Sylvia said she didn't know. She sat for a few moments waiting for the police and then remembered what she had found in the safe.

She quickly went to the same drawer in her father's dresser, finding the key and opening the safe from the closet. Gathering together all the papers and contents and tossing them in a Target bag that held some of her mother's items and rushed to her room. There was a secret space she had found in the ceiling of her closet that some prior tenant had made. Whether it was a space intended to hide drugs or what she hadn't known, but she'd thought it was a neat find. She dragged the nightstand over outside the door and standing on it she was able to reach and she placed the items inside and quickly dropped the ceiling piece back down. She had just returned downstairs when there was three hard knocks on the door and a gruff voice announcing the officer's arrival.

Chapter 9

T he female police officer was compassionate and had very kind eyes. Sylvia was grateful for that. She asked if she'd mind answering a few questions since it was imperative that the sooner they find out what she knew it could help find the killers sooner. She explained that the first 48 hours was the most important and everything she may remember could help them. Sylvia felt numb, this wasn't supposed to be happening. Will and Malinda had always been kind and loving to her, and even though she may have had doubts lately to whether they really were her parents or not, that didn't matter all that much at the moment. "Do you have a place to go?" the officer asked her. "I can go to my friend Amy's house," she replied.

The officer confirmed that it was the friend she had just been with and then asked if she'd like to go there now. She said she would, and she went to her room, gathering some items together she would need. She didn't want to even see Kaitlyn's things but had no choice. She thought of Kaitlyn's family being told she was dead and felt grief for them and even a small amount of guilt although she knew that none of this was her fault. The front of the house was already cordoned off and Officer Lisa Rodriguez lifted the yellow tape for her so she could go through. She got in the back of the police car, and the officer took a moment explaining something to the other two standing there. Sylvia assumed she was telling them about what she had learned so far and where she was taking her.

Officer Rodriguez got in the car and asked, "Are you holding up okay?"

She nodded in reply and then realizing it was dark and she couldn't see her nod forced herself to reply, "Yes," her voice croaked sounding loud in the car. "I'm so sorry, Sylvia; no one should have to go through something like this, ever." She put a little emphasis on the word "ever." She started the car, and Sylvia gave her Amy's address.

Amy's parents were very sympathetic, and Sylvia broke down in Mrs. Wooten's arms. She hugged and patted her telling her it would be okay and Sylvia wondered why people always said that. Saying it would be okay was a promise that no one ever had the right to say but still did. She knew there was really nothing else to replace those words and was sometimes all someone had to say.

She followed Amy to her bedroom, stepping over piles of clothing and books and countless other items strewn over the floor. Always before she had been amused by Amy's messiness, but now she was just annoyed by it. Malinda had always been fastidious with her housework instilling into Sylvia that cleanliness was important. She began stacking the clothes in a pile, sorting the pairs of shoes and pairing them together. It felt better to be doing something, and she knew Amy wouldn't mind or be offended. Sylvia suddenly began telling Amy everything, the words spilling out. All the years of doubt, the questioning, and not knowing who she really was began pouring out of her like hot lava, forced out by a desperation brought on by a broken heart and deep seated grief. She told Amy that she had hidden the contents and hopefully no one would find them. Amy listened with her mouth open in shock, and as Sylvia told how they had left the park that day so long ago when her mother had been so afraid, she shivered. They finally turned off the light and lay in the darkness. It was silent and still, and suddenly Amy sat bolt upright in bed.

She groped for the light and turned it on, the beam cutting through the darkness, casting it aside so only dark shadows in the corners remained. "Sylvia, I haven't met Kaitlyn, but you told me a while back that you both look alike," she exclaimed in a tense voice.

Sylvia sat up, pushing the covers back and sitting up against the headboard. "Yes, we do, or did." the reality of the past tense now applied shocking her once again. "Well," said Amy, "what if this wasn't just a random killing but people who really did finally catch up to your parents." Amy's voice lowered as she revealed the urgency of her thought. "What if that was supposed to be you they killed, and when they see the news they'll realize you are still alive?"

A wave of fear swept over Sylvia as the first time in her life the danger her parents must have felt now engulfed her as well. She instinctively felt that Amy was on the right track with what she said. "What do I do?" she asked. "If my parents really were in danger like I now believe they were why didn't they just go to the police, what was it they were running from that they could not have told the authorities?

Amy looked deep in thought, her round face troubled. She chewed on her lower lip and then said. "Whatever was in that safe may give us some clues, as soon as we can, let's go get it. Maybe they'll let us in by tomorrow afternoon and you can pretend you need a few things from your bedroom."

A while before noon the next day, the girls walked to Sylvia's house.

Sylvia had lain awake for hours, long after Amy had finally fallen asleep. Her mind had been on overdrive and wouldn't slow down no matter how much she tried. It was like the button was stuck and she felt like she was on a stretch of road heading for a dangerous curve, and even the steering was going to fail. And even when she had finally managed to doze off, she kept jerking awake, seeing her parent's lifeless eyes all over again.

The house was a two-story duplex, and her family had the unit on the right. No one was around when they got to the house, and the front door was blocked by yellow tape. Sylvia opened the door with her key, and they ducked under and entered. She had no desire to enter the room where her parents had lain, so she quickly walked past the doorway that would have led to the living room. Amy followed her as she went upstairs and she took the items from the hiding place. She had emptied her handbag at Amy's before leaving, so she would have more room for things. She put the items from the safe into her handbag, figuring if anyone would ask it would be less likely they'd look in her purse, and they'd be safer there.

Gathering a few more items, she filled the Target bag that had held the contents from the safe and then she and Amy left again. Neither felt like saying much. They walked back to Amy's house, and Sylvia thought ironically how the sun just shone. No matter what, through happiness or grief, the sun just keeps shining. She wondered if it would be easier if the weather would match her mood as it wouldn't seem like the cheery sun was mocking her sadness.

They arrived home, and Mrs. Wooten made them sandwiches. Sylvia sat at the table, woodenly chewing what she believed to be ham and cheese, but without looking she couldn't have said for sure. She ate because she was told to, and forced herself to eat the pudding cup that was on her plate as well. She excused herself and went to Amy's room. She took the handbag from the bureau, and sitting on the edge of the bed, she opened it and started looking through the items.

She found several yellow, small size manila envelopes and opening one, she found a VHS-c video tape and written on the front, in her father's writing, was 'For Sylvia'. There was a small note taped to it, that said, "Read Letter First." wondering what the video held, she lay it aside. Opening the second manila envelope, she found a thick wad of cash. The money was all in hundred and fifty dollar bills. Going through it quickly, she estimated there to be at least $10,000 in cash. She placed it back in the envelope, and put it with the video. She found the birth certificate and another envelope with her name on the front as well, but this one in her mother's handwriting. The envelope was sealed, and she carefully opened it. So much had already been torn from her within the past 24 hours, and it hurt to even tear the envelope. It held a single paper, and had been carefully folded in three. She opened it and began to read:

Dearest Sylvia,

I want you to know how very much we love you, your father and I. No matter what you view on the video, please know, even though you may not have been our daughter in blood, we could not possibly have loved you any more if you had been our biological daughter. You are special, always believe that about yourself. The first time I held you, I felt it. It was like a voice from heaven speaking to me and saying, "Watch out for her because I have great plans for her." We tried to do that. And along with doing so, there were times that we had to lie to protect you from the truth. A truth that is so harsh, we thought it would be best not to tell you. I ask your forgiveness. For the times in our protection of you, we know that you were hurt by the mistrust you felt. Please watch the video and find out what we tried so desperately to keep from you. Just please be careful, Sylvia. Be very cautious of who you trust, and always remember, whatever you do, there will be people looking for you. So make sure to never leave a trail for them to find you. If you are reading this now, then you will know that your father and I failed at doing so. We love you so very much Sylvia. Never forget that.

Love,
Mom and Dad

Sylvia lay on the bed and cried, clutching the letter to her chest. She now knew the truth, but knowing her parents really were not her biological parents, really didn't bother her as much as she had figured it might. She remembered all the special moments with them – Will clowning around, trying to make her smile when she was sad about something. Malinda always had time for her, no matter what she may have been doing. She just wished now, she had a few more moments with them, to let them know she held no anger against them and she loved them as much as they loved her. But that opportunity was gone, and she sobbed bitterly for a while, and somewhere in the crying and remembering, she dozed off for a few hours.

Sylvia woke and went to the kitchen and found Mrs. Wooten preparing dinner. She came to Sylvia hugging her and saying she was glad Sylvia had slept. "Would you like me to set the table?" she asked Mrs. Wooten.

"If you don't mind, you know where the things are." Sylvia pulled plates from the cabinet and placed them on the red checked tablecloth. She placed the proper silverware and tall glasses by each plate. When finished, she asked if there was anything else she could do.

"Not for right now, but she could help clean up the dishes later if she liked."

She said she would. "Mrs. Wooten, do you know if

you have an adapter for a VHS-c video tape?" "Is that the thing the small tape fits into so it plays in the VCR?" Mrs. Wooten asked. "Yes, it is."

"I don't believe we have something like that," Mrs. Wooten said, "But I'll ask my husband later." Though after dinner when they had the table cleared and in the dishwasher, Mrs. Wooten asked Mr. Wooten about the adapter and he said they did not have one. "What do you need it for, Sylvia?" she asked.

Sylvia had replied there was a video of her parents that she wanted to see, not going into detail.

Amy asked her parents if she could borrow the car so they could go to Walmart and get a new one. They gave permission and left soon after. Sylvia had taken a fifty from the manila envelope to pay for what she needed, and they returned an hour later successful in finding the adapter. Amy had a VCR DVD combo in her bedroom and told her she could watch it there.

Sylvia asked Amy if she would mind if she watched it by herself, and Amy said she understood.

Then Sylvia figured out how to place the smaller video inside the adapter so it would play and then inserted it into the slot. The tape flickered as it began, and then her parents filled the screen. Seeing them caused her to tear up, and she placed the video on pause for a moment, just looking at them.

Mentally preparing herself, she pressed play.
Her father began to speak.

"Sylvia, we love you. I hope you never doubt that." He looked at Malinda, and she echoed the same. He went on, "I'll never forget seeing you for the first time. You were so beautiful. We'll start from the beginning. Your mother and I were working at a biotechnology lab, where I was employed as a computer technician and your mother was a nurse.

The lab was doing testing on babies, and your mom worked the night shift caring for the babies.

"She grew suspicious of the testing being done on them, and she would see them become weaker and eventually saw their demise. She made some inquiries, and quickly discovered that questions were not welcome.

"It was actually after a veiled threat that she came to me with her concerns, and I began looking into it." Will paused, taking a drink of iced tea, and then setting it down, continued, "Thankfully, back then they didn't have the technology that is available now, and I didn't have to cover my tracks nearly as much. In my search through all their records, I finally discovered they were getting the babies through a smokescreen adoption agency that targeted young unwed mothers, most between the ages of sixteen and nineteen. It was then, they brought you in."

Her mother took over, her voice sad, as she explained how she was so taken aback by the new baby. "We had a baby who died, after living for only two weeks. I found her in the crib, and the doctors said she died from SIDS. They told us we couldn't have more children." Malinda swallowed, wiped a few tears, and continued. "When they brought you in, I couldn't believe how much you looked like Rachel. I asked Will to come see you, and although he wasn't allowed into where the babies were kept, we risked it. He also couldn't believe the similarities, and it was then, we knew what we had to do. We had to save you. They still had not begun any testing on you, but it was to happen soon. We took you that night. Your father got whatever information he could, and saved it to some computer files, which you'll find in another envelope. "We didn't know what we could do, so we ran. We went to Florida and settled there for a while. I would take you for long walks on the beach. And yes, it was in the park, you remember, I saw some men looking around, and I knew it was us they were looking for. It's one of those things you just know. After all those times of looking over my shoulder in fear, I just instinctively knew this one was real." Will placed his hand on Malinda's, and gently squeezed it. She took his hand and held it, finding strength from just having it in her grasp. "Sylvia, you have always been our sunshine, the one light in our world. Having you with us, has made all this worthwhile. And yes, even the dangers we faced were worth it. What we told you about growing up in foster homes is true. So, giving up families was something we never really had to do. How your father and I found each other is amazing, and together, we managed to put a life together. Your birth certificate is your own. It's real, and you can use it. Just remember that by surfacing with it, may place you in danger if they search records and see where you may use it to get a driver's license."

Her father took over again, "They know I have evidence, that even now all these years later, is still very incriminating, and can put them behind bars for a very long time. They will stop at nothing to get that back. They will be coming after you now that we are gone. Be brave, Sylvia. You are a very smart girl, and must do everything you can to survive. We've left you money in the envelope. We tried to save as much as we could over the years and that's what we've managed to put aside. Spend it wisely. We both pray that someday this will all be able to be over, and somehow these people will face justice for their actions. We also pray the deaths of all those innocent babies will somehow be avenged." Her father paused, and looked at her mother.

She looked back at him, and together, they looked back at the camera. Her mother spoke first, "Maybe someday you can find your birth mother. I know that often people regret giving their baby up for adoption, and maybe for you, this will be the case. In your father's search, he discovered your mother's name was Lenore Denton. She was only seventeen when she gave you up.

She believed their story; that you would be going to a loving home." Will said as the tape played. "She never imagined you'd end up in a lab, having illegal testing performed on you. We are so glad God brought you into our lives, and may He always keep you safe." Her father ended by saying again how much they loved her, and to have faith in herself and her abilities. The tape went snowy and the white and black dots flickered on the screen.

Chapter 10

Sylvia pushed the eject button and placed the tape back in the envelope. Now she knew what needed to be done. Somehow, she was going to disappear, and create a new place for herself somewhere. She would find someone that could create a new ID for her and would become an Amish girl and fit in there. Sylvia already knew that the lifestyle was something she could live with, and maybe happiness could come in the future. But now she had to concentrate on surviving, and that was one thing she had every intention of doing.

She didn't think she'd be able to get an airline ticket without having a proper ID, so she decided it would need to be by bus. But somehow, she was going back to see Lena, even if it meant hiding in the Bontrager's house and not surfacing again for ten years. But for now, all she could think of was the comforting arms of Mrs. Bontrager, and the love she would receive from Lena. She hoped they wouldn't mind if she showed up out of nowhere, but she had to take the risk. She had nowhere else to go. She went to find Amy, and together, they obtained a bus ticket for her to Ohio. The next bus leaving was at 3:40 AM, and they would take the risk that just by showing up an hour early, she could secure passage. She told Amy they should stop at Walmart and put $500 cash on a Visa card so she could spend it online if she needed to. Amy said she didn't want to ask her parents for the car, because they'd have too many questions. Instead, she'd just take the car and deal with their concerns later. A few hours passed, and finally the time had come to leave. Amy had agreed to take all of Sylvia's items, pack them in boxes, and send them to her at Lena's. She didn't know what she'd do with her clothes when they arrived, since she'd be wearing Amish dresses, but figured she could always store them.

They left, stopping at Walmart where she was able to secure the Visa card, and found the bus station. Although she felt reluctant to use her birth certificate, it was inevitable that it would be the only way to purchase her ticket. On the other hand, she felt fortunate this was all she needed for the purchase of her ticket.

Sylvia hated the bus drive. It smelled like someone had vomited, and it was only wiped up, never properly cleaned with soap and water. She didn't care very much for a few of the other passengers, and felt uncomfortable with the bold stares of a certain man. He openly stared, and would leer at her in a way that almost frightened her. When he finally got off at a stop in New Mexico, she was very relieved to see him go. She had been exhausted, but hadn't felt comfortable falling asleep with him nearby. A family of five clambered aboard just inside Texas, and even though they talked incessantly, she managed to fall asleep and slept until early afternoon. They were about an hour from Amarillo where she would be changing buses. She was ready for the change in atmosphere. She had a book she had grabbed at Walmart, but so far she hadn't been able to get into it. She hoped that later when the bus would be dark again, she could listen to music and fall asleep. She hadn't cared very much for the drive through New Mexico, and found Texas flat and boring as well. She remembered the beautiful green of Ohio, and wondered how soon they would be out of the brown, and driving through the green forests and open farmland.

After an hour and half wait in Amarillo, she finally changed buses, and was on the road once again. The bus was about half full, and she sat next to an empty seat. She securely placed her purse halfway under her, so if anyone tried getting to it, they'd have to pull it out from beneath her. Settling down with the headphones, she put on John Mayer and prepared to sleep. She woke up needing the restroom, not knowing how long it would be before they stopped. She went to the back of the bus where the small restroom was available. A sign at the front of the bus discouraged using it, unless it was an emergency, but she figured, "If not now, when?"

Returning to her seat and looking around, she noticed it was becoming daylight outside. The Ozarks were in the distance, and looking like a beautiful day ahead. She dreaded the long day of driving still ahead of her. She saw a sign that indicated St. Louis was coming closer, and she ticked off in her head the states left to go, Illinois, Indiana and then Ohio. They would be in Ohio late afternoon, and in spite of all the grief she had endured over the past several days, she looked forward to being with Lena and her family again.

She didn't know what would happen with her parents' bodies, and she hoped if they were buried, they'd have a beautiful burial site. She vowed to herself that someday she'd be able to come back and somehow have a memorial service of her own. But she knew that for now, she had to let that go. She had to harden that part of herself so she'd be able to survive. Will and Malinda were dead, she was alive, and she had to somehow go on. She thought of Lenore Denton who was her birth mother, but felt nothing. "Wouldn't you feel something by hearing the name of someone who carried you for nine months?" she wondered, but the name sat there in her head, unfamiliar and almost uncaring. The woman had given her up. What made her think she'd even want to know her? Maybe she'd just remind her of the worst nightmare of her life. She wondered at the circumstances that had caused Lenore to give her up. For a second she allowed her imagination to run wild, and then she reined it in. Telling herself to stop being silly, she tried to think of happier things. She felt hungry for the first time in several days, and rummaged in her bag for some packaged chocolate sandwich cookies she had found at a bus stop from one of the many vending machines. The cookies were wannabe Oreos, but didn't taste all that bad, and she felt better after eating them.

The day dragged by. She had picked up a variety puzzle book, at the same time she purchased the cookies, and that helped while the time away. They entered Ohio, and she knew it would be a few more hours before they got to Akron. She remembered her father working there when they had lived near the Bontragers, and remembered him saying he had about an hour drive to work. She planned on getting a motel when she got off the bus and then calling a taxi to take her to the

Bontragers. She had their address and figured the taxi driver would find them.

They arrived in Akron around 10 pm, and Sylvia saw a motel within walking distance. It was a Best Western, and she was soon settled in her room. She had a single suitcase and her handbag. She had been glad to get safely to her room. The walk had been longer than it had looked, and she was tired. She took a long shower, enjoying the hot water on her skin as it cascaded off.

The motel had a nice shower head, and it felt wonderful washing off the smell and dirt of the bus. She hadn't had a shower in 48 hours and felt covered in grime.

Although Will and Malinda had never been overly religious, they had still believed in God. They had instilled within her a deep belief in a creator. Even the times in school when she had been told differently, she hadn't argued but knew within herself what she chose to believe. She had given her heart to Jesus at Vacation Bible School when she was eleven, and even though she hadn't really known then what was happening, she had still known something had changed.

They had told her she could always trust in God and pray to Him for whatever needs she may have, but she had never really done that very much.

She finished with her shower and gave God some thought. She knew there would be a Bible in the nightstand drawer, placed there by the Gideons. She thought now would be as good a time as any to make reading it a habit. She needed all the help she could get and God was definitely one she'd give a try. She opened the Bible and saw a list of prayers on the inside. She saw if you needed help with fear, turn to Psalm 91 and so she did. Reading, how He would cover her with his feathers and she wouldn't need to fear the terror by night. It was a beautiful Psalm, and she felt herself comforted by the beautiful poetic words. She finished reading and placed the Bible back into the drawer, making a mental note to remember the chapter and book of what she had just read. She turned off the light and lay in the darkness, hearing faint noises from outside. She heard a car door slam, people talking, and in the distance, she heard sirens. She thought it ironic how life went on around you. It never stopped for anyone, even though she felt like her whole heart had been ripped out of her, the world didn't care. It went on in ceaseless mayhem, one day same as the next, just carbon copies of each other. Just the faces of the victims changed, as each person forfeited their rights to a happy world that had known no sorrow. She knew she would never take life for granted again, that no matter what happened, she would always treasure each loved one she'd have in her life. She fell asleep soon after, and slept deep and still. The sleep of those desperately tired, waking in the morning, to find her bed barely disturbed. Usually when she woke, her pillow could be across the bed, or on the floor or even on occasion at the foot end of the bed. She had always wondered how that happened. Will had tried to convince her when she was younger that little elves would come in the night and try to play tricks on her by stealing her pillow. But by the time they got to the foot end of the bed, they were simply too tired to go farther, and she should be glad, or else her pillow would be completely gone.

She took a quick shower, washing away the sleep from her eyes. She felt an excitement within her as she would be seeing Lena again. After eight long years, she'd once again be with the people who had always made her feel so special. She looked through the phone book, and finding a local taxi cab company, called and made arrangements. The earliest available would be in 45 minutes, so she thought she'd wait in the continental breakfast room. As she waited, she enjoyed a fresh cup of coffee and a bagel with cream cheese. She went to the desk just before the forty five minutes were up, and checked out so she'd be ready when the taxi arrived. She had been afraid if she checked out earlier, they wouldn't allow her the breakfast, so she decided to wait as she was embarrassed to ask the front desk clerk. The taxi arrived on time, and after the driver had her suitcase stowed in the trunk, she sat in the back seat as they headed out. She had given him the address and he told her that he knew exactly where that area was. He said there were several Amish stores he and his wife liked to frequent, and they would go there on occasion. He kept up a friendly chatter. Sylvia tried to follow along, and at least, give the appearance of having been listening. He said they were getting close, and she recognized the area, passing a barn that was set close to the road. She remembered that the next road past the barn was where they had always turned right, and Lena had lived down that road.

The cab driver slowed, making a right turn and the half mile went by quickly, and they were pulling into the Bontrager's lane. She paid the cab driver; he wished her the best and left.

Picking up her suitcase and purse, Sylvia walked up to the door that she had walked to so many times before. She couldn't remember a time she had not ever been glad to be there. There was something that she had loved about being at the Bontragers. She knocked on the door, and she heard someone from inside, saying in Pennsylvania Dutch, that there was someone at the door. She smiled as she heard the language again. She and Lena had often spoken it in their conversations together on the phone, and it had helped keep it fresh in her mind. The door opened and Mrs. Bontrager stood there. She looked just as Sylvia remembered. Her hair had grayed more, and her figure maybe a bit more ample, but the same kindness still shone on her face.

She looked at Sylvia for a moment, and just before Sylvia spoke, she said, "Sylvia?"

Sylvia nodded, her eyes welling up with tears, knowing she had recognized her, even without needing to be told.

Mrs. Bontrager enfolded her in her generous arms, holding her close. Sylvia found herself weeping. Mrs. Bontrager went to the doorway leading to the upstairs and opening the door she called, "Lena, come see who is here." Sylvia heard footsteps coming down the stairs, and there she stood, her friend from all those years ago. She could hardly see through her tears, but Lena rushed at her, and they both threw their arms around one another. Sylvia was openly sobbing, and Lena was crying as well. When they finally drew apart, they stood looking at each other. Mrs. Bontrager broke the silence, "Well, just look at you Sylvia, my, my, haven't you grown up into a beautiful girl." And it was true, Sylvia was a beautiful girl. Her light auburn hair was below her shoulders, and her makeup was perfectly done. Her eyebrows were finely arched, and with hazel eyes that turned green, depending on her mood. She had naturally beautiful teeth, and a well formed nose. When she was younger and had gotten into her mother's makeup, Malinda had not become angry, but told her that she would learn how to properly apply makeup and she'd teach her. So she had taught her, and told her, that too much makeup is worse than not enough, and there was the perfect amount for every face.

Mrs. Bontrager asked if her parents were also in the area, and she told them that they had both died. She told them everything that had happened and that she had nowhere else to go. She told them how sorry she was for being there and possibly endangering their lives. Mrs. Bontrager, again enveloped herself in her arms, assuring her that it was fine. She would always be welcome in their home, no matter the circumstances. Lena took her upstairs to her bedroom, and Sylvia asked her if she thought it would be better to dress in Lena's clothes, like she always had before. "You can wear them tomorrow if you like," Lena said. "It will be just like old times."

Sylvia already felt better being here. Even the sadness of her parent's death seemed more bearable. They talked about small things, and Lena caught her up on her older siblings and their families. Lena was the youngest of eight children, and the rest were all boys, except for one, much older sister, who was almost old enough to be her mother.

They finally went back downstairs, and Mrs. Bontrager commented it was almost noon. "What would you like to eat, Sylvia? Is there something special you remember that I could make for you?"

Sylvia thought for a moment. "I remember you would make something like a chicken and dumpling, but instead of dumplings you'd drop in fat homemade noodles, and it was almost more like a pot pie."

Mrs. Bontrager nodded. "Yes, then I will make that for our lunch.

When Sylvia protested that it may be too much work, Mrs. Bontrager looked at her and said, "You are like my long lost daughter who has come home Sylvia, please let me do this for you."

"Thank you, I feel like I've just come home," she said and tears began forming again. "Now, now," Mrs. Bontrager patted her on the back, "we'll take care of you again."

Sylvia sat and watched Lena make the dough for the noodles, as her mother was busily preparing the broth. She was amazed at the grown up Lena. She thought Lena was easily just as pretty as any of the girls at her high school, even with no makeup, and her hair neatly pinned up under her covering. She had tried to imagine what she would look like all grown, but how you picture people rarely ever is like you find them. In this case, she was more right than wrong.

Sylvia said she didn't want to impose on them for too long. She'd look for something elsewhere soon or come up with some plan. Mrs. Bontrager replied they would do some thinking and praying, and maybe they could come up with something.

They sat down to the delicious meal Sylvia had requested, and she thought it tasted just like she remembered. She ate like she hadn't eaten in a long time, and Mrs. Bontrager encouraged her to eat more, commenting on putting some meat on her bones. Lena laughed, and said it was a wonder that she herself had managed to stay thin, because her mom was always saying that to her as well.

They spent the afternoon just enjoying being together. Later, they went out to the garden to help Mrs. Bontrager pick green beans, and then came the time sitting around on the patio snapping them.

When they finished, it was time to begin dinner, and soon Lena's two older brothers, still living at home, made their appearances from their day working construction. Sylvia felt almost shy around them, since they had been several years older than she and Lena. They had never liked having two small girls tagging along behind them. During dinner, she noticed Daniel, the younger one, kept stealing glances at her and realized it may become uncomfortable living there if it would be like this every meal.

Mr. Bontrager had been surprised and happy to see her, and expressed sadness for the death of her parents. He had welcomed her into their home, echoing the words of his wife, by saying she was welcome anytime.

Chapter 11

They had a sumptuous feast of baked chicken, mashed potatoes, gravy, canned corn, and thick slices of homemade bread then topped off with apple pie. Although Malinda had been a fair enough cook, nothing she had ever cooked tasted quite like this, and Sylvia ate until she felt uncomfortable.

The feeling was not familiar, and she didn't like it, telling herself that in the future she'd be more careful, no matter how good the food was. They washed all the dishes, put them away, and then went outside and played a game of croquet with Daniel and Martin. Lena whispered to Sylvia, "It's because of your clothes that they stare at you like that. They'll stop once you wear Amish clothes." Sylvia hoped so, and couldn't wait to look like Lena so the stares would stop.

They played until dark and then sat around a fire that Mr. Bontrager had built in a fire pit. Lena said, "This is a favorite pastime for us in the summer and fall before it gets too cold," Sylvia commented that she had never done this much, as there had always seemed to be burn laws in Arizona where it was illegal to build a fire because of the chance of wildfire.

That got the family started on asking her questions about Arizona and her life. They spent the next while talking about life there. Finally, when it got to the point where the mosquitoes became too unbearable, they arose and went into the house. Lena lit a lantern, and they went to her bedroom. Giggling together, they went through her closet, and Sylvia picked out a dress to wear the next day. Lena gave her an extra white covering she had. They lay in bed talking, and finally when their eyes grew heavy, gave in to sleep. Sylvia was still not used to the three hour time difference, and could have slept longer upon waking the next morning, but got up anyway, looking forward to the day.

Lena had to show Sylvia how to fasten the front of the dress that was secured by pins. It wasn't like the little girl dresses they had worn that fastened in the back. "Why can't you just use buttons?" she asked.

Lena shook her head. "It's one of those things that was decided, and we've always done."

Sylvia thought for a moment and asked, "But do you ever wish you could have buttons instead of pins?"

Lena smiled. "Sure, all the time, but there is really no point in being unhappy about something that is unlikely to happen. So why not just choose to accept it and be happy?"

Sylvia was struck by the simplicity of that answer. In a world that lived by "show me the proof and I'll believe," she was amazed that people lived by such a simple rule, willing to see past their own desires to have what they considered the best interests in mind for all of them.

The girls got dressed and went downstairs. Mrs. Bontrager stood at the sink, "Good morning girls," she said cheerfully. Sylvia greeted her back, and Mrs. Bontrager said, "Sylvia, we talked it over and believe we may have the perfect plan for you. Somewhere you can live and be safe."

Lena asked her mother what that was. "Lena, we hadn't told you before, but your uncle Paul in Michigan, had asked me if I would consider letting you move there and help them in their bulk food store," Mrs. Bontrager said. She paused and got a pleased look on her face. "But your father and I talked it over last night, and we wonder if this isn't the perfect answer for Sylvia. They have an apartment above the store that they have fixed up and have it furnished. What do you think Sylvia, is that something you may consider?"

Sylvia didn't want to think of leaving the Bontragers so soon after just arriving, but she knew their safety meant more, so she agreed that it did indeed sound like a good idea.

Mrs. Bontrager went on, "Have you also considered that you'll need a new name? Maybe that is something you can think about, and Lena can help give you suggestions.

Sylvia looked at Lena, and she nodded and said, "We'll work on a name later."

They ate breakfast, and then Sylvia helped Lena do the laundry, hanging out basket after basket of fresh-smelling laundry. After the last of the clothes had been hung on the line to dry, they washed windows and then went to the garden, pulling the few weeds that had dared make entry through the soil to peek at the efforts of Mrs. Bontrager's green thumb. Sylvia loved working in the soil. The simple toils the family put into living their life may have been physical, but she felt a satisfaction knowing that through her own efforts a few green beans that would be eaten that winter, would have come from her own hands. They discussed names as they worked in the garden, and finally came up with Sarah Ann. Lena told her that Abraham's wife, Sarai, had a name change, too, and God changed it to Sarah, which was a Hebrew word meaning princess. Sylvia liked the name, and they added Ann. Lena said they would give her the most common Amish surname of all, and this way, she'd blend in better. So her full name became Sarah Ann Miller.

Sarah Ann moved to Michigan two days later. Lena had shared some of her clothing and promised to immediately sew some more and get them sent to her. She met Paul and Miriam Mullet, and knew from the start, she would enjoy working for them and living above the store.

Paul was a good natured man, with a cheerfulness that matched that of his sister. His wife was a sweet, quiet spoken lady, who never raised her voice. She made Sarah Ann feel welcome, and made sure she knew if she needed anything, all she had to do was ask. They had six children, three boys and three girls. Sarah Ann liked working in the bulk food store, and along with grocery items, they also sold small gifts and some crafts that other local Amish made. She didn't know how she was going to answer all the questions that would be sure to come. Her salary included her living quarters, and her pay wasn't really that much, but she didn't need much to live on, and she began adding to what her parents had already saved for her.

They had built up a nest egg of just over $12,000 and

she had spent almost $700 for bus fare and moving. She knew her parents had saved the money in the event they would need to once again make a sudden move, and she was determined to always do the same. She tried not to think of the fact that as far as her life seemed to be going, she would not be finding a boyfriend anytime soon. Who would wish to enmesh themselves into such a mess?

Life built itself into a routine. Sylvia was just happy she was able to even have a stable life. She missed her parents, and there were moments she deeply grieved for them. At times, she would cry herself to sleep with a loneliness that was bone deep. She had always been a happy girl who liked to have a good time, and friends had always said she was the life of the party. But now, only a shadow of that girl remained. And maybe it was the sadness she carried, that kept people from prying. But the questions she had feared would be asked, really did not happen that much. For that, she was grateful, and she determined that if she was going to be Amish, then she would strive hard to be a good one.

Amy's parents had taken care of all her things and sent them to the Bontragers as she had requested. She had called and specifically instructed Amy to save certain special things of her parents. She then sent enough money for two years cost of a storage locker to Lena, and they had placed all her items into storage for her. She didn't know why, at the time, but she just wanted to know everything was where no one could get into them, and she had felt a storage locker would accomplish that.

Months passed, and before she knew, a year and a half had gone by. The Amish lifestyle had become normal and comfortable to her, and she really didn't want to leave. She was slowly beginning to be the happy girl she had always been. She thought of writing once again. She had not felt like it for a very long time, but she had just opened a box of merchandise for the store and found some lovely hardbound journals. She bought one, but as the day was a busy one, and she had things to do before a youth gathering at the schoolhouse the next day, she wasn't able to get started immediately. A small settlement, from another part of Michigan, was coming by invitation to spend the day with them. Saturdays were usually a busy day at the store, but Paul and Miriam had wanted her to take the day off so she could spend it with the young people. Sarah Ann felt that she should pay them back for their kindness, and out of gratitude was working longer on Friday..............

*****

Allen settled down to read the last of Sarah Ann's writings. This one was a journal, a hardbound book with a nice floral pattern. This was something he could have envisioned her choosing, and one he would have picked out for her as well, had he given it as a gift.

His mother had just sent it to him. She and his father had found it under the mattress of the bed Allen and Sarah Ann had shared. The weeks had passed, and it was now almost seven months since Sarah Ann had passed away.

He was still saddened, but was slowly learning to accept her death. He still had moments where it seemed like he felt her presence, but he wouldn't hold on to them anymore, like he had at one time. He opened the book and began to read, and then stopped, as his mind grasped what he had just read. This book began precisely the day she had first met him. He knew that now he'd finally learn what he really meant to Sarah Ann. He only hoped her love for him matched what he had felt for her.

*****

..........I met someone today. Someone quite like I've never met before. I'm afraid that I may have been a bit forward though, and something I may have said, could cause him to think poorly of me. I guess it was easy to revert back to a life that I had spent for so many years, and I simply forgot that most Amish girls wouldn't be so bold about making their interests known. He is good looking enough, but it was more than that. He carried this presence. It's difficult to explain, but if I had to explain what it was, I'd say it was a self-assurance and a confidence, but with no amount of cockiness. He stood there at first base, and I wanted him to notice me. But he didn't seem to, so I said something really dumb, and now he probably thinks I'm an idiot. I don't know why I should even care anyway, it's not like I would be able to do anything about it, even if he did like me back.

I could hardly believe it when Miriam handed me a letter that came today. I don't get any mail, since the only way Lena and I communicate is by phone. It was something we thought would be better, in case anyone was watching their mail. It was from Allen Gingerich, I hadn't known his last name, so was kind of confused as to who it could be.

Imagine my surprise! I guess he hadn't been turned off after all. He asked if he could come see me and if I thought that would be a possibility, to please reply, either way. I am in a war with myself right now. My head is saying no, but my heart is screaming otherwise. I'm going to wait a week before I reply, I really should just say "no" now, and save myself the heartache later.

I sent my reply today and told him it was okay to come see me. But wait, I did tell him to not expect anything, because I'm not looking. I know, who am I kidding, right?

He wrote me back and said he'd be coming to see me next Saturday. Now that it's really happening, I'm so excited, but also scared. I've never dated an Amish guy before. How different can he be, men are men, women are women, right? So why am I still so apprehensive?

Oh, I guess it could have something to do with, someone trying to kill me, but other than that, it should all go fine. I know, sarcasm isn't funny. But my life really isn't funny, and why not be sarcastic about it? Is it too much to wish for a normal life right now? One where I could just enjoy learning to know someone I am very interested in?

Allen will be coming tomorrow. I can hardly concentrate, and I've told myself a dozen times that I should have just said no, but it's too late now.

I don't even know where to begin. If there has ever been a definition of a perfect date, this was it.

There's a beautiful lake about a mile from my house, so I packed a lunch for us, and we walked there. He listened to me, like every word I was saying was meant to be treasured.

He told me about his parents, how he grew up an only

child, and like me, always wished for siblings. He works in masonry. I wasn't sure what that was, until he explained it to me. I thought it had something to do with bricks, and I was right. He liked the bulk food store and bought a few things to take home to his parents. I thought it was nice of him to remember them. He asked if I'd like to see him again sometime soon, and I said I would. I more than want to!

Today made the fourth time I've seen Allen, counting the first time, when I thought I'd made a disaster out of everything. He told me he is beginning to have deep feelings for me. I told him that I felt the same, and I realized if I didn't tell him the truth, I never would. I kept silent knowing I would not turn back now, and was crossing a threshold into something I may regret later.

The Amish do things so differently. He explained to me that in some of the Amish circles, dating isn't considered a very serious thing, and casually dating lots of people wasn't unheard of. But the Amish settlement he was from encouraged courtship. You didn't date until you felt that your attraction for someone was inspired by God, and only then did you venture into a courtship. I don't know how to feel about this since it's so different than the world I came from. Just the term courtship seems so antiquated, but the way Allen sounded when he told me about it made me feel so special. Like I was more than just a passing fancy, and he had put a lot of thought and prayer into "courting" me.

Something has happened to me, and I don't believe I shall ever be the same again. I think I'm in love, no let me rephrase that. I know that I am in love. I have fallen for Allen in a way that I didn't even know existed. He is in almost every thought and I can hardly concentrate on my work.

Tomorrow will be the eighth time we see one another, and I am going to meet his parents. He told me that I will like them. But doesn't every guy in the history of the world say that, and how many end up actually liking their mother in law?

I admit it. I may have been a little foolish with my fears. His parents are every bit as nice as Allen said they would be. His mom is a wonderful cook. She made the most fabulous meatloaf and pies I've ever tasted. His dad is an older version of Allen, and I can see Allen being just like him someday. I believe I could learn to like having them in my life all the time.

Allen proposed to me today! When I was younger I'd dream about how I'd be proposed to. The wildest proposal I imagined was in the middle of a stadium and people viewing it on the big screen. Or another was in the middle of an airport, like in so many endings of movies. But this was so different, so simple yet so perfect. I wouldn't change one glorious moment.

He asked me to take a walk and so we did. We walked down a long lane, that at one time was a path for cows. Part of the way, alongside the path, grew wild grapes, and we got to a small meadow where almost right in the middle, was a big tree. When we got there, to my surprise, there was a small folding table and two chairs, and an ice chest with food, complete with a tablecloth and a sparkling cider. I could not have imagined a more romantic moment. I had just taken a mouthful of trail bologna, Swiss cheese and a cracker, when he proposed. I almost choked on the dryness of the cracker, so great was my surprise. He was saying how much his life had changed since he met me, having me in it, gave it more purpose and he couldn't imagine not having me be a part of his future, and then just asked if I'd like to be part of his life forever. "Will you marry me?" he asked. I said yes, well, I said yes, after I stopped choking, that is. He had also told me how his church discouraged much physical contact before marriage, so I wasn't expecting anything, but he gave me a gentle kiss on my lips. It was more of a soft brush that lasted a mere second, but had it been a minute, it would not have been enough. I can't wait for the day when his ideals of "courtship" are over and we can indulge in a much longer kiss.

Since the Amish don't wear jewelry, there will be no ring adorning my finger to announce my news. But I do believe the joy on my face may just be able to do the same. I am not the same person leaving his home than I was when I arrived that morning. He doesn't want to wait very long to be married, and I agree. I didn't tell him, but it's not like I have anything holding me back. Other than what I haven't told him, but I meant sending out invites and things like that. I have no one to invite.

Even though there is one snag, I am not a member of the Amish church. A person has an opportunity to join church twice a year by going through the articles of faith. It's right after communion, either in the fall or spring, that classes begin, and since it is early fall now, Allen said we could get married in about five months after I am baptized. I am a bit put off by the formality of everything, but I would do anything to be with him, so I will approach the bishop of my church and tell them of my intentions.

Chapter 12

...**M**y first instruction class started today. It was rather interesting but almost embarrassing as well, since right during the service I had to get up with three others and go to the basement where the ministers were waiting to counsel us. I could feel all eyes on me, and I already dread the next one in two weeks. I am taking this seriously though, and even if I'd do almost anything to be with Allen, I want this step in my life to be one that God is a part of as well. I have asked Miriam to help me learn some recipes and she's been showing me. Learning to make pie crust is a struggle.

Who knew a perfect pie crust would be so difficult to make? I finally mastered what I think is acceptable, but I still want to improve on it. I want to be the best cook I can for Allen.

I have two more instruction classes left, and I have learned so much. They were actually rather interesting. They are called the articles of faith, based upon the beliefs of Anabaptist Christians who later became known as Amish and Mennonites. It's been interesting learning about Anabaptist history, and Allen has been answering my questions. He gave me a book owned by his parents, called the Martyr's Mirror. I don't really care that much for it. It has some gruesome stories of people dying for their faith. I only hope I never face that choice.

Sometimes I wonder where that girl went. The one, who only several years ago had a sociology degree in mind. It's kind of strange how things that seem to matter so much one day seem so inconsequential the next. Life is so bittersweet, though; I find myself at times missing my parents so badly, but in spite of all that I found Allen, and somehow it seems my heart is healing. I can only pray, that what I fear most in life will not rear its ugly head and drive us apart. I am not sure I could survive if I had to suddenly leave him. I don't think life would be worth living anymore, and I'm not sure I can bear giving up so much, again. I've lost too much already.

We will be married in a little less than two months. We'll be living in Allen's parent's upstairs for a while until we find a home of our own. I'm a little apprehensive, but I've learned to really care for Amanda. She and Dan are both very sweet to me, and always make me feel welcome when I am there.

I felt like pinching myself today to make sure I'm awake. Life is so beautiful and I'm so happy. Almost three years have passed since my parents were so brutally murdered, and yet, I have been able to find happiness once again. I know they would be so happy for me. I don't think they'd even mind that I'm Amish. My mom always said, "How we feel, so are the things that we do." Basically, that means, happy people, do happy things. Kind people do kind things. But that isn't to say, we can't make ourselves do nice things, even when we don't feel like it.

It's nice to be able to do those things because they

come from a state of happiness, and not forcing myself to act only because I know it's the right thing to do.

Allen and I are not having a large wedding. I have no one to take care of the arrangements, so his family will be having church that Sunday, and we'll marry at the end of the service. Instead of the traditional after church meal, we will be serving a full wedding dinner for each of the guests. Which will be baked breaded chicken, mashed potatoes and gravy, several vegetables, a bread stuffing, dinner rolls and, of course, cake and ice cream. And if you know the Amish, of course, there will be countless pies. A feast by anyone's imagination. I asked Amanda if it wouldn't be too much work, but she insisted, so I gave in.

Not having a big wedding doesn't matter as much to me as I would have thought. I'm just so glad to have Allen in my life that everything else seems so trivial in comparison.

Sewing is still a struggle for me. It's something Miriam has been teaching me, but it's been a slow process. I am able to sew a dress well enough for everyday use, but I wanted my wedding dress to be special. Miriam said she'd be glad to sew it for me, and she finished it last evening.

I was so pleased when she presented it to me. It's a little darker than the traditional royal blue color for Amish brides. It's a beautiful soft knit, and like the color, I felt almost royal when I tried it on for the fitting. It fits me perfectly, and it's about all I can do in making myself wait for my special day when I can wear it and know Allen and I will be one.

I finally get baptized today. I am sitting in the early hours of a Sunday morning, realizing that today is a big step for me, and even as I am writing this, reality is sinking in. I will be making one of the greatest decisions of my life, and one that will bind me to the Amish church forever. When you look at it that way, it seems so foreboding. But unless I take this step, there is no Allen, no us, and I don't want to live without him.

It really wasn't as bad as I had feared. The baptism went well, and the people were so kind. I was so blessed by the kindness and love I have experienced from them, and they welcomed me in as a member yesterday. Our wedding is now only three weeks away.

My wedding is tomorrow. I am excited beyond words, but I can't help but feel a certain amount of sadness as well. I find myself missing my parents so much, and wish they were here to share in my happy day. Allen explained how an Amish wedding is performed. It doesn't seem very warm. Every girl imagines her father walking her down the aisle, and I had always pictured my day as one where I'd walk down the aisle on Will's arm, and my beloved standing at the altar with a smitten look on his face. The way the Amish do their weddings is another thing that I have to accept, and realize, that another dream has to be laid aside. I will make the most of it, and accept that it's only a wedding, and the marriage that follows, is really what matters most.

We've been married for a week now, and I can't imagine being happier than I am now.

Allen is everything I could ever have dreamed of a man being, and his love for me is almost overwhelming.

I haven't shown him this journal, nor do I have any intention of letting him see.

When I have this filled, it will be sent to Lena to place with my other items in storage.

*****

..........Allen smiled as he read about their first year together. Sarah Ann had written about small moments they had together. At the time, they had seemed trivial to him but reading them now he realized how much they had meant to Sarah Ann.

*****

We celebrate our first year together, and I am making Allen a special meal.

Knowing the meals Amanda prepared for him before I came into the picture always made me feel inferior, even though I know he would eat my cooking no matter how unappetizing it may have looked. I love him, even more for that, and I have tried so hard to improve. I know my cooking has drastically improved and I feel like such a better wife than at first.

Once, he did tell me that what I lack in cooking I make up for in housekeeping.

A clean house is important to him, and always has been for me as well.

Although the time here with his parents has definitely been more than bearable, I believe every couple needs their own space and I am looking forward to our own home.

We've been looking for our own to call home, and Allen seems to think one place in particular may be promising.

Saturday, Allen will be going to a sale with his dad. I plan on staying home and catching up on a few things.

This will be my final entry in this book, and then I will be sending it off to Lena. There is something I have not told Allen. Among all the other things, this is a secret that I don't intend on keeping long. I am pregnant and it's news that is bursting from me. I can hardly prevent myself from telling, but I am waiting for that perfect moment………...

*****

Allen lay the book down. It ended there, and he sat stunned, shaken to the core, by what he had just read. Sarah Ann had been pregnant. He took a while to absorb the grief and sadness that flooded through him. He calculated in his mind that had Sarah Ann been living, she would be having the baby in about a month.

If there was one thing he had learned over the past months, it was that you couldn't change certain matters just because you wished for them to be different.

Now that he was done reading about Sarah Ann and all he had learned about her life, he wondered if he would ever learn the truth about what it was that had kept her family living in such fear. He rose from his chair and placed the book in the box with the other diaries.

In spite of the sadness, he felt some assurance in the knowledge that the love she had for him was real, and he believed what she had written. He also thought of the fact she had never had time to get the journal sent off to Lena, and it was only because he had told his mother to go ahead and rent out the space to another young married couple, that they had found the journal.

Allen rose the next morning determined to be the best teacher he could be, and as the week wore on, he wondered how long it would be before he felt like pursuing a love interest elsewhere. He was missing the companionship and didn't like coming home to an empty house each evening. But he didn't want to rush into something just because of loneliness. Doing something rash may only lead into regrets he would have to live with for the rest of his life. Amish married for keeps, and after the love he had shared with Sarah Ann, he couldn't imagine going through another marriage with anything less.

He watched Ada Marie as she coached the first graders on their "schwa" sounds. She was so patient, and he had marveled at how much time she had taken with one certain boy who had such difficulty distinguishing long and short sounds. He knew Ada Marie represented the perfect example of what an Amish woman should be, and he knew that given time, he may even be able to have feelings for her. He turned his thoughts back on his duties and told the seventh graders to get out their geography books. Soon the day ended, and shortly thereafter, he had locked up and was on his way home.

He met Amos as he was on the sidewalk leading to his house. "Hello, haven't seen much of you this week," Amos said, cheerful as always.

Allen replied, "I've been catching up on some reading."

Amos thoughtfully stroked his beard and said, "I'm always here if you need anyone to talk to Allen." "Thank you, I appreciate that," Allen said, wondering if the events in his life were that obvious to others. "Oh, I almost forgot, there's some mail for you. Let me go get it for you." Amos went into his house and returned shortly, handing Allen his mail. Allen thanked him and went into his part of the house.

One was from his mother with more magazines and another long letter with news from the neighborhood to keep him updated on current events of life there. He enjoyed reading about the people who had been such a vital part of his life. The other letter did not contain a return address, and his name and address was typed on the front. It was postmarked Columbus, Ohio, and he wondered who he would possibly know from there. He knew it had to be somewhat important because not many people knew he was staying at Amos's home. He gently opened the envelope and pulled out the folded letter. It contained two sheets of paper, and as he opened the letter, he nearly fell from shock as he recognized the handwriting. He looked at the top of the page to see when it had been written and saw it was dated only seven days prior. His heart was pounding furiously, so hard it felt like it would pound its way right out of his body. He turned it over, his eyes roving the page desperately seeking a signature and there at the bottom of the page, he saw her name: *Signed with all my love, Sarah Ann.*

He wondered who would play such a cruel joke on him. He staggered to his chair and sat down, holding the paper to his chest, as if too afraid of what more shock would already do to his overworked heart. He willed himself to breathe, slowly calming himself and then when he felt able he lifted the page and began to read.

Chapter 13

My Dearest Allen,

These past few months have been so difficult for me. Knowing you believe I am dead has me going crazy that I can't tell you the truth, but until now I couldn't.

Yes, I was struck by a car. I woke up in the emergency room, and they came there to make sure I was dead. I heard them asking about me by the front window, and they were told they couldn't come back there but they came anyway. It was all I could do to drag myself from a bed where I lay broken and bleeding but somehow I managed. I had enough foresight to grab my medical chart and as I went through another curtained room desperately seeking a way out, I saw a very bandaged young lady who was hardly recognizable and I quickly exchanged my chart with hers. I threw hers in the trash bin outside. I am not proud of what I did, but when you are faced with death, it's amazing what comes to the forefront and what vices you will use to survive.

I have found a place where I am safe for now. I am sure they have discovered that I'm not dead. Lena told me that there was no body viewed at the funeral. I am not surprised, as she was very disfigured.

Allen, I love you with all my heart. I won't ask you to come to me. I won't ask you to live the life of my parents, where at any moment you may need to pick up and run. I don't know if you found the journal I left under our mattress. If so, and you've read it, you will have known some other news I was about ready to tell you. Amazingly, I didn't lose the baby in the accident, and if everything goes well in a month or so you will be a father. I have not been to a physician because I don't want to give any information to anyone, but everything seems to be going well.

I want you to come to me with every fiber of my being but I will not ask you to leave what you have always known and matters so much to you. Your Amish faith is everything to you.

I know you will recognize what is on the other paper and if you do decide that a life with me is what you choose then everything you need to find me is on that paper. Just be very careful and if you do decide to not come to me, please destroy it.

I love you Allen, you matter more to me than life itself and it was for you that made me drag myself out of bed that day. Had it not been for you, I would simply have given up.

With all my love,

Sarah Ann

*****

Allen reread the letter and laid it aside. He was still reeling but within him came a slow awakening to the realization that Sarah Ann was alive. "She is alive!" he thought excitedly. The thought crossed his mind if it could possibly be a cruel joke being played on him, but as he picked up the other paper he knew immediately that it could not have been written by anyone other than Sarah Ann. The paper held two columns of words, each word was five letters. Beside each word was a number, the numbers ranged from between zero through three. It was the Five Letter Game he and Sarah Ann had played so often during their short time together. She had skillfully figured out a way for him to come to her and his finding her all depended on his ability at solving her words. At the bottom of the page she had written a short note asking him to bring her jewelry box.

Allen wondered what to do. Did he leave everything he had ever considered important to him for Sarah Ann and his baby or would he stay knowing everything within would want to be with her now that he knew she was alive? He thought of Amos' offer to be there to talk to if he needed someone and thought he would possibly take him up on it. Whatever the decision would be, it would need to be made quickly because he couldn't take any more of the suspense that had become part of his life. All that he'd discovered wasn't something he could just put behind him, and he thought of all the long months of grief he had endured. How do you go from that to knowing it was all for nothing. Not that he didn't feel joy at the knowledge of knowing she was alive, because he did. It was just all so confusing for him, and right then he felt like going crazy. For the first time ever in Allen's life, he felt like cursing at life, how it had placed him in such a quandary of needing to make a choice that would hurt others no matter what the decision would be that was made. His parents would ultimately be hurt, and it was at that moment he knew what he would do. He'd go home, and his parent' would know the right thing to do. He couldn't remember a time in his life that their faith and wisdom hadn't solved whatever matters that had come up.

Allen arrived at his parent's home late the next evening. He had found a ride quite easily and the chunk of money it had cost didn't matter to him. He had needed to find someone who was able to transfer all his things and also Sarah Ann's boxes and cartons from the storage unit.

He had also told Amos as little as possible, not wanting rumors to fly and Amos had said that he'd try to take care of matters that would prevent that from happening.

Allen didn't feel good about the decision to leave his teaching position but saw no other way out of it, there was no way he wanted to wait another six months before deciding on what to do.

He noticed a light on in the kitchen window and saw his father standing in the doorway.

Seeing the familiar figure almost made him break down in tears, but he bravely smiled as Dan held the door wide for him to enter bearing his heavy load. He placed it down and gave his mother a big hug. They both wiped tears as they separated and he turned to his father. Shaking his hand in a hearty grip, his father laid his hand on his shoulder. His voice choking as he said, "Welcome home, Allen."

He hurried out the door after telling them he'd be right

back and making a few more trips back and forth he soon had everything inside.

He then turned to the questioning eyes of his parents knowing the questions would now come.

Why was he home without warning?

His mother was first, "Allen, is something the matter, did you have a falling out there with the school? He shook his head and his father calmly said, "Amanda, give him time. He'll get around telling us soon enough." "Do you have any hot coffee mom?" he asked.

Amanda shook her head but quickly said, "I'll make us some." Turning to the stove, she soon had it lit and was heating water.

Allen said, "It's a long story and you will have a difficult time believing some of it. But I'm telling you now that it is all true and I've come home for advice."

Dan pulled out the kitchen chair and motioned Allen to sit down, and sat down himself. He cleared his throat. "Why don't you start from the beginning, tell us what it is that has caused you to leave and come home to us. What is it that is so unbelievable?" He had begun by telling them that Sarah Ann was alive.

He saw in their faces what his own must have looked like.

His mother got up and stumbled to the stove, woodenly preparing the coffee. Her ability to do so relying on her hands to somehow do what they had done so many hundreds of times before.

Allen finally got done talking, telling them everything he knew.

Once again his mother spoke first, her voice breaking

the silence. "What will you be doing, Allen?" Amanda's voice softened as she said, "You are having a child, we are having a grandchild."

Allen nodded. "I know, and I am too shocked to even know how to feel about it."

Amanda said, "Allen, a baby is never a bad thing. Sometimes decisions made in how a baby is planned for is not such a good thing. But in this case, nothing was done in a way that you should look back on with regret. Sarah Ann is the person I knew her to be. I really believe that."

Allen was so glad to hear his mother say that; it was how he felt about her as well. "But what do I do?" he asked.

"You will go and bring Sarah Ann home," Dan said firmly.

Allen was relieved to find his family so supportive. But he knew that the next information he would relay to them would not be met with such approval. "I have thought it over, and I believe the only way I can go find her is by leaving the Amish to do so." He paused and then continued quickly before either of them could object. "I will be much more conspicuous than if I were not. I don't know who is trying to find her but I need to do what I can to make myself less noticeable."

His mother managed to look even more shocked than she had yet and his father scratched his beard thoughtfully and then said. "I think too going as Amish would be more conspicuous; it's just that for me to say it's okay for you to leave is something I am not sure I can do." He went on his voice sounding old and tired and very sad. "I, however, am not going to stand in your way, Allen, I just ask that when you somehow get things worked out to when it is safe to come home, that you would do that. You and Sarah Ann live a life here with us like you did before."

Allen had never loved his father more than he did at that moment. He reached over and clasped his hand and squeezed. His father squeezed back, somehow in that small handshake giving back all the love he couldn't have given in a hug.

Standing up, Allen drained his cup and placing it in the sink he told them good night and then stopped before he got to the door that opened to the stairway. "Where do I sleep?" he asked, suddenly remembering that they had rented out the upstairs. "I have a guest room prepared in my old sewing room," his mother told him, "You will sleep there. I wasn't expecting you to use it so soon, but I can't say that I'm not glad."

Allen slept well enough, the bed was his old one from upstairs so it was familiar and he had often missed it while being away.

He rose the next morning, and his mother prepared him a large breakfast. He ate hungrily, appreciating the work that had gone into preparing it. He had missed his mother's cooking but hadn't realized how much until he was eating it.

Allen knew that before he could set out on finding Sarah Ann he had to first solve her clues.

He sat at the table and began. It had been a while since he had played, but he remembered well the rules. He spent a long time on the first column, and when he thought that he had finally come up with the word, he wrote it down and went on to the next. It wasn't that easy and he had run out of words to make it simpler, had he been playing in person he could have asked for more words but that wasn't possible so he had made do with what he had. The last one he finally figured out had to be a word formed with the letters R.E.L.O.T. He wondered if that was a word by itself and getting the dictionary he found it to not be a word. He tried T.O.L.E.R. but still to no avail. Finally, he tried O.R.L.E.T. and looking it up in the dictionary he found it to be an actual word.

Placing it with the first word of S.T.A.I.R. he went to work solving where the location could be that Sarah Ann would be hiding. He assumed that the last two letters would be the state and the eight preceding letters would be the town. He tried all kinds of variations beginning with taking away the last two letters what he knew could possibly be the state. After working for several hours on the clues, he took a break. His shoulders were tense and sore from being in the same position for so long.

The familiarity of home was doing him wonders, though, and he thought a walk in the crisp air would help clear his mind so it wouldn't be so befuddled, and he'd be able to solve the puzzle and learn her location.

So he put on a coat and his hat and went out past the barn and walked down the lane and through the meadow where he and Sarah Ann had spent the special date and where he had asked her to marry him. He sat under the tree smiling as he remembered her choking on her cracker. How her face had lit up and she had said yes.

He felt excitement at knowing he'd be seeing her again

soon and resolved to work harder at finding her than anything he'd ever done in his life. The thought of a baby excited him as well, even if the setting for being a parent had not been what he would have imagined or created for himself.

He sat a while longer until the chill in the air began setting in, then he strolled back to the house.

His mother was baking his favorite cookies when he walked in the door, and he had smelled them before even entering. She placed a few in front of him along with a fresh cup of coffee.

He thanked her as she patted him on the back and went back to her work.

He once again took up the pencil and went to work, placing letters together as he tried to make some sense out of them. He suddenly wondered if he took an atlas and looked at it state by state if it might be of some help, all the while knowing it would be a long and tedious job.

He began with Oregon, glad it wasn't a very heavily populated state and continued to Arkansas and when still having no luck, he began to feel discouraged as he moved on to Illinois. That state was full of towns, so far the most populated of those he had tried, and it was when he had thought of looking in the index instead of on the map itself that his finger suddenly stilled."Could it be?" he wondered, all the letters fit. Streator, Illinois, population 13,000. It seemed like a difficult task but one he was willing to take on. Going on gut instinct, he felt it was likely where she was. Not terribly far away but still far enough to have some distance. He felt good to have something to go on and now that his decision was made he knew it would be happening now and not later.

Allen didn't want his parents to see him after he'd shaved his beard and been to a barber.

It would have broken their hearts to see him any other way than how they had always known him.

He knew getting a driver's license would not be that difficult for him since like many Amish boys the thrill of knowing what it would be like to drive was a lure most could not resist.

He had driven plenty of times with a friend who had kept a car hidden during his rumspringa years, and his friend had taught him to drive. It would be a simple matter of passing the written test and waiting whatever amount of time it was that they allowed a driving test to be taken. His heart pounded as what was in store for him began settling in. Although he had never desired to leave the Amish, the curiosity of what another life would be like out there was exciting him much to his surprise.

He left the next morning, driving his horse and buggy. His parents had taken care of the horse for him while he was gone. He enjoyed driving a buggy and the drive to the nearby town where they had a license bureau ended too soon. He tied up at a neighboring store that had a hitching rail and walked over to the license bureau. He felt awkward asking for the information on getting a license since it was obvious from the curious looks he was receiving that not many Amish came in for this purpose. He was told he would need to wait two days in the state of Michigan before taking the driving part of the testing for his license. He felt exasperation and asked how long a period of time was required in Illinois and after she willingly looked it up online told him there was only a short wait. She asked him if he still wanted the Driver's Education Booklet, and he took it. He could study it on the bus on the way to Illinois.

Allen's mind was racing wildly as he made his way back to the buggy. He would take the bus to Streator, get himself established with an address and get a driver's license and car there.

One thing he was grateful for was how his parents had instilled in him the wisdom at spending his money wisely. He had a nice amount of savings that he and Sarah Ann were going to use as a down payment on their new home. But that could wait, and it was available for what needed to come first.

He drove home and after telling his parent's he was leaving first thing in the morning, proceeded to go to the phone and make some calls. He found someone to take him to Grand Rapids where he'd take the bus to Illinois.

Chapter 16

Allen bid his parents goodbye the next morning. It was a much more subdued goodbye than he had ever experienced before and he sensed an underlying sadness in both of them. Although neither one of them said anything negative about his intentions he knew they were still more concerned than they were letting on. He found a motel in Grand Rapids and was grateful that it was within walking distance of stores. After securing a room, he walked to a hair salon that boasted Men Women and Children on its front window. He walked in the door, aware of the stares that met him. He almost turned and ran, but he had come so far there was no turning back now. There would be a fifteen minute wait he was told, after giving his name and sitting down he looked at a magazine. Seeing a book on haircuts, he picked it up and leafed through. Most of them were cuts he couldn't imagine on himself and shuddered at one that had a strip of hair that fell forward over one eye. He decided to get a regular haircut, like the picture of the man on the wall. He liked the nice clean look and admired how it was cut over his ears.

His name was called and he went back to the chair she was indicating and sat down. After she had the black apron tied around him and he had explained what he wanted she started to cut. Thick chunks fell as she cut and he was unsure how he felt. He had never done this before, and it was never as obvious as now. Christina – the name on her name tag – was chatty and asked him more questions than he could hardly keep up with. "I've never cut an Amish man's hair before," she told him. "It's all the same, hair is hair," he replied.

"Very true but I still think it's cool."

She snipped around his ears and he cringed inside hoping she wouldn't cut him in all her talking. She finally finished, and he looked at himself in the mirror, she held a smaller mirror behind him so he could see the backside. "I like it very much," he told her with a smile. He thanked her and paid, unsure if a tip was required and thought he'd give her several dollars just in case. She took the tip as if it was an expected thing, so he was glad he'd listened to his instincts.

He walked out, his head feeling light and the breeze going through his much lightened hair.

He wasn't wearing a hat, as well, and that felt almost as odd as the new haircut.

The department store wasn't very far away, and he walked down the sidewalk feeling like a new person. The beard would go next, and he reminded himself to find something to take it off. A small pair of scissors to get it short enough for a razor would do, he decided. Allen found the Mens clothing section and began looking at the jeans. They had Wrangler, and it was a name he was familiar with; holding a pair against himself he estimated the waist to be close to fitting him and saw a fitting room. He went over and was told which room to go to. He tried them on, finding them to be a little loose. Trying the next smaller size, he found them to fit him comfortably. He bought four pairs in several of the different colors and then looked for some shirts. He was finding it difficult to find something too bright or striped and tended to lean toward more sedate lines and tones. Finding a few T-shirts he liked, one had a Nike swoosh on the front and the other was a deep blue one with a small silhouette of a man fly fishing with a grizzly bear in the background. He moved to the long sleeved and found a gray pinstripe on black that he found that he liked and went well with the black pair of jeans he had found.

He moved on to the shoe's aisle and found a nice Adidas white with a gray stripe that was very comfortable. He had always liked this style of shoe and had one in black, but the white was something he'd never thought would be part of his wardrobe.

He winced as he thought of how much it would all cost. He went to the personal care section and found a small scissors. He had brought the toiletry items with him from home but remembered the toothpaste tube was low, so he added a new one to his growing pile.

Going through the checkout, he chose a magazine for the bus ride and after paying for all the items carried them all back to the motel.

He was hungry but thought he'd shave off his beard before going to eat. Standing in front of the mirror, he looked at himself, knowing in a few minutes a new image would appear. He clipped off the hair as close as he could and then lathering up he shaved it all off, leaving short sideburns like he remembered seeing in the picture.

Taking a quick shower, he got dressed, pulling on the

new clothes after removing the tags. He stood looking at himself in the mirror. He didn't look like the same person.

He walked out of the motel and going to the street, looked both ways. Seeing a sign for a Denny's next door, he walked over. He was shown to a booth and looking through the menu he decided on just a regular old cheeseburger and fries. The waitress took his order and left him to sip his coffee and wait on his food.

He noticed several girls watching him from a corner booth. He wondered why since he wasn't dressed in his Amish clothes anymore, but then the realization hit him they were noticing him for his looks. Being stared at because of being Amish was a familiar thing, but being noticed for his personal appearance was an entirely different matter. He wasn't sure how he felt about that and wished he'd be left to eat unnoticed. He was glad they left soon after, and the section he was in had no one else other than an elderly couple who were talking quietly with one another. He ate in silence, and when he was done eating, left a generous tip and rose to leave.

He got back to the motel and after laying on the bed turned on the television. He thought, "I may as well live it up." He watched a tennis match for a while, but he found all the talk confusing and the scoring with love didn't make much sense as well so he moved on to something else.

He settled on a "Mutual of Omaha's Wild Kingdom" and soon found himself enthralled by the lives of a pride of lions. The show had just begun and lasted for an hour and then he moved on to "Law and Order." It was a show he had read a story about in Reader's Digest when the magazine had featured a story on of the main characters. He had thought then it seemed like an interesting show, but had never thought it would be something he'd be seeing.

It wasn't long before he was glued to the story, his mind racing as he tried to determine whether the suspect being held in question was really innocent as he claimed.

The story had a surprising twist at the end, and he realized then that it was a show he wanted to see more of. When the announcement came on to stay tuned for more "Law and Order" and that it was a marathon, he was glad.

He watched two more episodes and then found his mind too heavy to pay attention to the show and after nodding off twice he finally gave in, turning off the television.

Brushing his teeth, he remembered to pray, and crawling beneath the sheets thought if he was fortunate sleeping alone would be ending soon. He hoped to have found Sarah Ann before the baby was born to be present at the birth so she'd not have to be alone.

The bus wasn't leaving until 10 a.m. so he had no need to rush in the morning. He drifted off to sleep and woke the next morning feeling refreshed and ready for anything the day had to toss at him.

The bus was on time and pulled out promptly at ten. Allen had arrived well over an hour early to make sure he wouldn't miss the bus if it chanced to leave early. He hadn't thought it would be very likely that would happen, but he wanted to be prepared just in case. It was scheduled to arrive near Streator in a city called La Salle.

From there he planned on taking a taxi to his destination. He suddenly realized that he hadn't even bothered to find out if Streator had any lodging but assumed in a town of thirteen thousand the odds were good they should have. The bus was fairly full, and he sat next to a nice older lady who told him all about her hip replacement. Allen was sympathetic and it was all the encouragement she needed.

She didn't just stop with her hip but also told him of her knee surgery the year before.

She droned on, and he found himself thinking of other things and would need to bring himself back to answer and fumble at words to make sure he had the correct responses.

He had once again looked at himself in the mirror that morning and marveled. He was aware that it was something that he'd take a while to get accustomed to. Always before, the times he'd traveled on the bus, it would be next to someone who without meaning to would ask personal questions about the Amish that he'd find invasive. People seemed to think it was alright to ask anything they had a question about, and he had been asked some strange questions in the past. Wearing non Amish clothes was a relief as it allowed him to blend in with the other passengers.

The day wore on, and he pulled out the driver's ed booklet and began studying it. Most of the things in the book he had already known. Amish may not be required to have a license to drive on the road, but they were still required to follow all the laws and the signs were familiar to him.

He had always been attentive when a passenger in a vehicle on highways, so the signs were not new to him as well. He felt confident enough to take the self-test at the back of the book and found he had aced every answer. He had gotten them all correct and knew that he'd soon have his license.

The bus had a quick stop, and he grabbed some food; when he got back on board he had the seat to himself since the elderly lady had gotten off there. He had helped her with her things, and she hadn't been able to stop expressing her appreciation and saying what a nice young man he was.

He found a motel in La Salle and called for a cab in the morning to take him the short distance to Streator. He found there were indeed several places offering lodging, so he made reservations for the next evening at a place called The Birdseye View. He hadn't known mountains existed in Illinois. The name sounded deceptive since he assumed with an impressive title like that it would be reserved for a mountaintop lodge but still chose it because he liked the name.

He found out later the next day upon arriving that it sat on top of what he'd call a knoll and it was a stretch of the imagination to call it a bird's-eye view.

The room was acceptable enough, but the heater groaned and moaned until he finally got up in the middle of the night to turn it off. He chose risking freezing to death over the noise that thing made.

He woke to a somewhat chilly room and turned it on long enough to take the chill from the air.

He ate breakfast at some nondescript little restaurant

where the food was so greasy it almost made him nauseous, and halfway through he stopped eating. So far his stay in Streator hadn't impressed him at all and he realized he really wasn't even positive Sarah Ann was in the town.

He told himself to stop doubting and just search like he believed she was. It would be a better thing to put his whole heart into it than leave it to chance that she wasn't.

*****

She was so tired, every bone in her body seemed to ache, but none as bad as her back.

Still two hours to go on what was left of an eight-hour shift. She was so tired she had to concentrate on just putting one foot in front of the other. She smiled wearily at the couple who had just been seated at a booth and took their drink orders. The weather outside was so dreary that the customers needed all the cheer she could give them. And cheer was in short supply these days.

She knew that time was running out and in less than a month the baby was due. She was beginning to despair that Allen would find her in time. Sarah Ann didn't want to believe he may have just simply chosen to not come find her but that was a thought she had been in denial about.

She sighed as a group of noisy teenagers came in and took the corner booth. She had nothing against teens, other than they were poor tippers and couldn't seem to eat without leaving her a big mess to clean.

The decision loomed in front of her, and she had told herself that if Allen didn't find her by the time the baby was born she was going to be giving up the baby. The only bright spot she had seemed to be able to find was the knowledge that going by how it made herself feel, if her own birth mother had felt the same way then she at least would know that she hadn't just been a baby someone hadn't had the time for and just been tossed aside.

Sarah Ann thought of the dingy studio apartment she was renting. A single room with a small bathroom, one so small it seemed a disgrace to call a room. The shower was so tiny and she had gotten so big that she'd begun dreading taking showers. The upside to it was the low rent, and she hadn't wanted to touch the money her parents had left for her. So far she had been able to leave it alone and manage to live off her tips. She finished her shift and made her way home, which was another good thing about the dump she was living in, it wasn't far from where she worked. She didn't care for some of the people who loitered around the area and was sure that drugs were probably being sold right under her nose. She figured though what she didn't know wouldn't hurt her and minded her own business. Walking through the door into what she was calling home never filled her with much hope, and that was another thing along with cheer that she didn't seem to have much of anymore.

Chapter 15

Allen found the license bureau, and to his great happiness found they had a kiosk from which he could take his written test. Many places only offered classroom tests and those were only on certain days. He found to his satisfaction he only had one answer incorrect. Walking out with a temporary driver's permit he'd been told that he needed his own vehicle for the road test. They suggested he call a driving school, and he could use their car. So when he got back to the room, he called and made arrangements, and they agreed to pick him up the next morning. He went to the office and asked if they could possibly give him a room with less noise and after paying for two more days, got settled in a similar room that to his relief was much quieter.

He woke the next morning and after walking to the corner service station brought back a ready-made breakfast sandwich and some hot coffee. He had an hour before they would be picking him up for his driving lesson and road test. They had told him the price was the same whether he used them for three hours or one so he decided he may as well brush up on his driving skills.

He'd also be needing to either buy new clothes soon or do some laundry. He'd seen a laundry room as he was walking by down the hallway from his room, so he thought he would get to that later that evening.

The driving instructor arrived just before nine, and he left to take his test; when he arrived back at The Birdseye View, three hours later he had completed what he'd set out to do.

The instructor had been amazed that he'd not had a license before and told him he should pass the test with no problem and he'd been right. Allen did pass with a perfect score.

He walked to the used car lot and within an hour was driving away with a five-year-old Chevy Malibu. It was a four-door sedan with tinted windows. It was nothing fancy, the mileage a little higher than Allen had liked, but everything was working and he didn't see any car repair bills in the near future. He decided to chance the short drive to the motel without insurance but made sure to get that out of the way as soon as he got there.

Looking in the Yellow Pages, he found nearly forty establishments that dealt with food services. Writing them all down he got started, taking along the photo of Sarah Ann he had received in the first letter. He managed to make it to four that day, no one had recognized the photo. He found another place that served food that was not on the list. They, too, had not seen her.

He was on his third day and becoming discouraged. He had spent his whole day before going from one place to the next inquiring and then asking directions to the next place. It was a slow way of going at it, and he wished he knew the area so he could just drive to it. He'd wasted so much time backtracking.

He had just been seated in the early afternoon and ordered his drink when he saw her. It was a family-style café, and she had just walked through a pass way that had an open section. He had been studying the menu, and it was by chance he had looked up and saw her walk through. His heart stopped, and it was almost all he could do to not get up and yell her name. When the waitress came to take his order, he told her what he wanted and asked if she'd tell the other waitress that he'd like to speak to her.

*****

"Lauren, there's someone at booth seven that would like to see you."

She looked up still not use to hearing the unfamiliar name. "Is it a man or woman?" she asked hesitantly. "Man, and a good looking one at that. If you don't get out there soon, I will."

Sarah Ann peeked through the pass through and could just see the side of his face. It really was him. Allen had found her. But this wasn't like any Allen she had known before. This one had a haircut that was definitely not Amish.

A wave of love swept over her as the knowledge of what he had given up for her washed through her:

Allen was really here!

She slid into the booth, and they clasped each other's hands. Staring into one another eyes they both had tears running down their cheeks. She spoke first. "You came, you really came."

"I married you for life, Sarah Ann, and you are my life," he told her, his voice throaty with emotion.

The waitress brought his plate of food and set it down on the table." So you really do know each other," she said, then sensing the mood wasn't light she turned away, saying as she went, "All the good looking ones are always taken anyway."

"You look so different, like you're not even the same guy," Sarah Ann smiled tearfully." I am though, maybe not on the outside but still the same on the inside." Allen smiled back. "How much longer do you need to work?"

"I get off in an hour."

"Who do you tell that you won't be coming back again?"

"I can just leave a message for him." Sarah Ann said. "Payday was yesterday, so I'm not losing much if he does decide to be vindictive that I quit without notice."

"If you can bring me coffee, I'll just wait the hour here until you get off."

Sarah Ann glowed. It was like someone had turned on a light bulb inside her. For the first time in days, she felt happy and there was something else she was feeling. It was hope, she realized.

Allen was not able to take his eyes off her, drinking in the sight of her like a parched man who couldn't get enough water for his dry throat. He also couldn't stop looking at her stomach, amazed that their baby was inside.

The hour passed, and he led her out to the car. He had not told her about it yet, and she squealed when she saw it.

They drove to her small apartment, and she gathered the few things together she had accumulated the short time she was there. Thankfully, it had been furnished, and although the furniture hadn't been overly nice to look at, they had been serviceable.

They went back to The Birdseye View, and he carried her over the threshold. They still had a lot of serious talking ahead of them but somehow for now they just wanted to be with each other. Making up for all the lost months.

They woke the next morning, so happy to be together. It seemed like a dream to both of them and they lay in bed talking.

Allen told her about reading her diaries and how sorry he was for the loss of her parents.

She broke down then and told him all about her life. How she had spent so much time with the Bontragers and also her life in Phoenix.

After she had told him everything she possibly could remember to tell him, he was especially curious about the video her parents had left for her. "Do you want to find your birth mother?" he asked her.

Sarah Ann thought for a while and then nodded. ""I really believe I do, before my parents died

I'd have said no. But now, there's such a big part of me that wants to meet her and have her tell me why she gave me up."

Allen nodded understandingly." It's having my own baby and knowing how desperately I wanted to keep him or her that has made me aware as well that she may be living her life longing for a day that I would someday find her."

Do you think we can find her?"

Allen pondered it. "What would be the hurt in trying?"

"Let's do it then."

They got up, and each had a shower. Sarah Ann enjoyed the much larger shower and took a long, welcome one. Feeling so refreshed by the full night of sleep, for once not waking in fear from dreams that constantly hounded her. The hot water washed over her and she felt renewed. She smiled at herself in the mirror, realizing the tired and sad woman from the day before was barely recognizable in the now fresh face of hope. She was happy, so very happy, and she felt so protected. "It's what the love of a good man should feel like," she thought.

She marveled at how good looking Allen was with his haircut and new clothes, though she had never minded the way he dressed and thought he was handsome in Amish clothes as well.

They had breakfast at a nice little diner that specialized in breakfast. Sarah Ann ate like she hadn't eaten in a long time. She had lost her appetite along the way and had forced herself to eat for the baby's sake. They discussed what they would be doing that day. "So we know her name was Lenore Denton, since that was what your parents told you," Allen said thoughtfully. "And she was from Florida, at least that's where my birth certificate is from."

"That's a good start," Allen said, "At least something to go on."

"We could find a library and start there," Sarah Ann suggested. "I could go online and see what we can find."

"Sounds good, we'll ask for directions to the nearest one before we leave."

They found the library with very little difficulty and

were told to sign in and were given a half hour.

"If it's not busy in a half hour, you may sign up for another session," a very bored looking librarian told them. Even though it was a library and quiet was thought to be mandatory, she cracked her gum like nobody's business, and Allen thought he'd go crazy. When someone asked for her assistance, she finally dragged herself reluctantly from her desk to assist them. Allen sighed with relief for the short break she gave them.

Sarah Ann typed the name into the search bar and the search engine revealed several results but none were from Florida. "What if we just hire a private investigator?" Allen asked. "

It's not like we don't have the money. I do not have the slightest idea at how to go about finding someone, but finding missing people is their specialty."

Sarah Ann started the search for a private investigator and located several in Bloomington. Writing down the information of two of them that looked promising, they left the library. It had begun to snow lightly and they held hands on the way to the car. Again, Allen opened the door for her." You don't need to do that for me every time."

"I know I don't, but I want to." "Then who am I to stop you?" She laughed." We should stay on the move for a while anyway," Allen said. "At least move often enough to make sure they won't find us."

"Is there something we can possibly do to get ourselves out of this mess?" Sarah Ann asked. She was softly tapping her fingers against the side window as Allen drove to Bloomington.

They had loaded everything from the motel, and she said goodbye to the city of Streator with no desire to return."

There has to be someone we can go to for help, we can't just live our lives being hunted like rabbits by some..." She hunted in her mind for the proper word. "...some beagles. But in this case beagles carrying guns."

"Something is telling me the key to all of this is finding your birth mother." Allen paused. "I don't know why, but it just seems the appropriate thing to do."

"We'll need a cell phone in case the investigator finds anything, and you will need more clothes as well," Sarah Ann said decisively.

They stopped at a Walmart just outside the city limits, and purchased a "pay as you go" cell phone that didn't need a verification to have it activated and they could use any name they wanted.

"What do you think about this?" he asked Sarah Ann, as they sat outside a rather nondescript brick building. The building was in a sad state of decay, the mortar chipping out from between the bricks. The wood sign, Fred R Dolan P.I., was faded, the red paint long having given way to streaks of whitish gray. The office was upstairs with a wrought iron stairway leading up to the door. "We drove this far, let's at least check it out," Sarah Ann said, opening her door.

To their surprise and relief, the stairs were more solid than the rest of the building indicated they would be. They stood on the small landing, and Allen knocked on the door. Though it was a business, it just seemed they should knock.

An indistinct holler was heard from inside; guessing it was a summons to enter, Allen opened the door. The room was about 20 feet square and there was a window on each side of the building. Both windows had old fashioned shades hanging haphazardly and halfway down. The dreary light tried valiantly to pierce the sadness of the room, but did hardly more than peer in through the dirty panes of glass.

The desk sat smack dab in the center of the room and behind the man seated there was a sofa positioned so the TV could be watched from where it sat in the corner. The television was the old kind with the turn knobs and it was tuned to a game show.

He rose from the desk and walked over and turning one of the knobs shut off the TV.

Had anyone drawn a figure to go with the surroundings, it would have been of this man. His hair stuck out in all directions. He was bone thin, and his ears were large and his nose bony.

Sarah Ann's first thought that came to mind was Ichabod Crane." Allen stuck out his hand and greeted him, "Mr. Dolan?"

He grunted in acquiescence as if the question seemed ignorant to him like the sign on the outside didn't already inform them of that.

Allen went on as if his rudeness wasn't noticeable. "Mr. Dolan, I'm Allen Gingerich, and this is my wife Sarah Ann. We spoke on the phone."

"What can I do for you?"

"His voice surprisingly pleasant sounding. So far, it seemed his only saving grace.

"We are trying to locate a person and wondered if you could help us with that," Allen told him.

"It's my birth mother," Sarah Ann chimed in. "We are trying to find her."

"I see," he said rather languidly then squinted. "Do you folks know how many people come in here looking for either children or birth parents and there is nothing that can be done for them?

In many cases, unless the birth parent – which is the case here – has requested the files be opened, it is literally impossible to open them unless you are prepared for a long and costly court procedure." He saw the disappointment in their faces and his own softened slightly. "And then in that case, it wouldn't be me you'd be needing, but a very good attorney who specialized in those kinds of cases."

He motioned for them to take the two chairs that were placed across from his desk and they sat down.

Allen leaned forward. "So if you did take all the information we gave you and Sarah Ann's mother had indeed opened the case in the likelihood that she may be looking for her..." He looked at Sarah Ann. "...you're saying the odds are more likely that she would not be opposed to meeting?"

Mr. Dolan nodded his skinny neck. "That is what I'm saying, but I am not a mind reader and have no way of knowing what a person will do. Who is to say that even though the files were opened, when the time comes they may still say no. It could prove to be too much."

"How much is your fee to find my mother?" Sarah Ann asked him. "You will begin with a retainer fee of one thousand dollars. That may or may not be enough to cover my time and expenses. I will let you know if more is required."

She looked at Allen and he nodded. She dug in her purse and pulling out some bills, counted ten hundred dollar bills to him. He counted silently as she gave them to him, his lips forming each number.

Although he was almost comical looking and seemed like nothing they'd ever expected to find they knew the search for a private investigator ended here.

Giving him all the information they had, he made copies of a few documents and after giving him their new cell number they left.

Chapter 16

"**I** know he's strange as can be," Sarah Ann remarked once they were in the car and leaving, "but I like him."

"Yes, me too," Allen agreed. "Let's find something to eat; I'm getting hungry."

"Okay, what sounds good?"

They finally settled on looking for a chicken place and as luck would have it, found a Kentucky Fried Chicken just several blocks down the street.

Having eaten their fill of chicken and everything that came with the meal they went on to find a place to stay. They found a clean looking and budget friendly single floor motel that had a lit up vacancy on the sign.

Allen took the things inside and they spent the evening playing the five letter word game and watching television. Both still could not get over the fact they were together again.

Especially Allen, since he was the one who had believed for all that time he'd never see her again.

Sarah Ann woke in the middle of the night, her heart pounding. She had heard a car door slam and some voices outside. She crept out of bed, careful to not disturb Allen. She could tell by his breathing that he was in a deep slumber. She moved to the window, enough light from outside shining around the hanging drape to show her the way. She carefully pulled the one edge of the curtain aside, just far enough to peer outside. Two men stood at the backside of a car by an opened trunk. She could hear their low voices and as she watched, a woman came out of a room adjacent to theirs and they finished their conversation, closing the trunk and following her inside.

She didn't want to spend the rest of her life like this, always starting at every noise and waiting for evil to find them. She hoped and prayed that Mr. Dolan aka Ichabod could quickly find her mother. She went to the restroom and after washing her hands stood at the sink looking at herself in the mirror.

Her stomach large and round, and she felt the baby move inside her, a foot kicking, and she put her hand on where it was pressing.

Her heart filled with such love for the little being inside her. The desire to protect her unborn child rose up with a fierceness that almost shook her.

She turned off the light and made her way back to bed. She gently lifted the covers and slid back into bed. Snuggling up to Allen's warmth she slowly drifted back to sleep.

*****

Several days later, and Allen had called Fred Dolan asking if he had learned anything. There was a short conversation with Mr. Dolan informing him that he was still waiting on a friend to call him back, but he would let them know as soon as he knew anything.

By his tone it was clear that no phone call from him meant no news, and would be pointless for them to call. They had no choice but to be patient and so they whiled away each day, reminding each other that life could be worse. They could still be apart.

Allen especially was becoming restless. Since completing the eighth grade, he always had a job, and sitting around every day was about to drive him crazy.

Several more days passed, and they were in the middle of discussing baby names. As late afternoon approached, every name the other suggested didn't seem to strike their fancy. They had finally written down several tentative ones when the cell phone rang. They both jumped at the unfamiliar sound and then grew excited realizing that it could only be one person.

Allen answered, and it was the private investigator. He was calling from a cell phone, and the reception was very poor. It wasn't clear enough for them to learn much information. So he hung up after arranging for them to meet the next morning at nine.

They stopped at a quaint little German style bakery the next morning and each had delicious apple strudel. Sarah Ann thought it would be nice to buy several for Mr. Dolan as a nice token of appreciation. They once again made their way to his dismal looking office and presented him with the strudel.

He expressed his appreciation for their thoughtfulness and after receiving the information they needed, went on their way to find Sarah Ann's mother.

They were headed toward I-70 and discussing the information they'd received from the private investigator when the cell phone rang. Allen recognized the incoming number as Mr. Dolan. "Hello," he answered the phone with a query in his tone.

Mr. Dolan greeted him back, his voice strained. "Allen, are you stopped or driving?"

"We are driving."

Mr. Dolan told him in a voice that sounded urgent, "When you get to an exit, please pull off and call me, it is very important."

"Sure, we will do that." Allen replied, hanging up he related the conversation to Sarah Ann. "What could be wrong now?" she wondered aloud.

Allen turned off at the next exit and seeing a small strip mall turned in there.

Mr. Dolan answered on the first ring. "Allen, a few minutes after you left, several guys came in here. I've been in this business a long time and I know 'bad" when I see it. They held a gun to my head and told me if I don't give them all the information I have on you they'd kill me and my family."

Allen had put the phone on speaker so Sarah Ann could listen, and she audibly gasped, her hand going to her mouth in horror. "We just missed them," Allen realized.

"Yes, thank God I had your number on my phone from my call yesterday," Mr. Dolan said. He went on, "I know good people as well, and you are both good people. They know where you are headed, so I think I have the solution for the time being. I have a cabin in the Ozarks, and I'd like for you to go there for a while, at least until it's safe to move on."

"We also have the baby coming soon," Allen said. "Maybe we can wait until after Sarah Ann delivers and that will give us a little time to get something planned out."

"Yes and it probably won't be safe going to a hospital either. Normally I'd never recommend having a baby outside of one, but I know someone who may be able to help you."

He stopped, taking what sounded like a swallow of something, and continued. "It so happens that the corner market by the cabin is operated by a retired nurse. She has been friends with my wife and me for many years. I will call and talk to her about matters, let her know you'll be coming there and she'll look in on you."

Sarah Ann spoke out for the first time, her voice shaking with emotions that she was having difficulty keeping in check." Mr. Dolan, we don't even know how we can thank you for all of this." "No thanks are needed, he said gruffly. Just be careful and I hope everything turns out for the best for the two of you."

He went on to give them all the information they would require which included the address to the cabin and the location of the key. "Just make yourselves at home and eat whatever you find there."

Allen and Sarah Ann were overcome with the kindness of someone that at first glance you would underestimate and never expect the graciousness he so very well knew how to extend.

They ended the call and sat in shocked silence for a few minutes.

Finally, Allen turned the key and said, "You never know from one moment to the next how things can change. I am learning that planning our day is not something really possible anymore."

"I know," Sarah Ann agreed. "But at least we have a plan for now anyway."

"Yes, and we may as well get started." Allen turned to the back and straining to reach pulled the atlas to the front. He turned to Illinois and looking carefully figured out the best way to get to the cabin.

Sarah Ann started singing a Christmas carol as they drove along. It was difficult to imagine that in the midst of it all the holiday season was upon them. The baby was due on the 23rd, and they had both agreed that she or he was indeed the only present they'd both need.

Just several weeks ago, it was barely imaginable they would be together with a new baby. They basked in the knowledge that soon they'd be parents. They arrived in Missouri that evening and found a nice hotel. Allen suggested spending a little more on one that would have a hot breakfast, and they settled on a Holiday Inn Express. It was definitely more than they had been paying, but Allen pushed the concern of the price away and paid for it anyway. They settled in and were both pleased with the comfort of the room.

After enjoying a hot breakfast in the morning, they sat over steaming cups of hot chocolate and talked.

"I really believe God has a specific plan for each of us," Sarah Ann said, sipping her hot chocolate. She delicately wiped her mouth with the napkin. "What amazes me most is how he uses unlikely people to fulfill that plan. To think, we considered not hiring Mr. Dolan due to his appearance."

"No matter how nice he turned out to be, the building still needs repair." Allen smiled. "But that is just because

I was a mason, and the sadness of that brick building is what I saw first."

They both noticed a family of four and the mother gently cradled a young baby that could not have been more than a few months old. They smiled as realizing very soon that would be them.

Rising, they rose to leave, and after Allen had checked them out and loaded their bags, they headed for the cabin. It looked to be only about twenty minutes away, and they were excited they would not have to stay in a motel and would settle somewhere for a while, even if only for a few weeks.

They turned off onto a side road, that although paved, was narrow and had lots of sharp curves.

Mr. Dolan had told them the cabin backed up to a lake, and they passed a sign that read two miles and pointed them toward the lake. There was a rather dilapidated old store on the corner with a "General Store" sign above the front window. It had a lighted OPEN sign that shined feebly above the door. There were no cars in front of the store, just an older pickup truck parked to the side.

"That must be the store Mr. Dolan mentioned," Sarah Ann said. "Business must be slower during the off season." "We can come back later after we are settled," Allen said turning to the left, as the arrow on the sign indicated. They drove a half mile passing several driveways they assumed must lead to hidden cabins not seen by the dense foliage. Even though the leaves were all off the trees, the underbrush was still so thick that visibility inside the forest didn't extend very far.

Chapter 17

They finally found what they believed to be the right place. It had the broken off stump that was just before the driveway that Mr. Dolan had told them to look for. Allen drove up the driveway and stopped by the front of the cabin. From behind the structure they could see the lake. From where they were standing and by what they could see, it looked beautiful.

Allen walked to the side of the house where the fireplace was located. Counting up eleven bricks from the bottom, he located the loose brick that was the third one from the left. It lifted away, and he found the key that Mr. Dolan had told him would be there. Placing the brick back into place he went around to the front and unlocked the front door.

The cabin was simple yet serviceable. The kitchen was to the right of the door, and the dining area extended to the living room. The fireplace was on the side and there was a single bedroom and a bathroom, and though not very large still, had all the required amenities. There was a small loft above the bedroom with a ladder on the side leading up to it. The rest of the room was wide open with a cathedral ceiling. It had a deer head above the fireplace and a chandelier made up of antlers hanging over the dining room table.

It was mostly a man's cabin, but you could still see a

few feminine touches here and there. The blue gingham curtains hanging over the sink had a frilly lacy edge by the hem and the table held a nice dried flower arrangement.

Allen expressed his approval of the place, and immediately after bringing everything into the cabin set to work on building a roaring fire. The place was cold and looking around, they found a small electric heater that helped heat the bedroom area where the fireplace didn't quite reach.

They opened the refrigerator and found it empty, but the freezer was stocked full.

They found a room that was built onto the back of the cabin. It didn't allow entry into the cabin and you had to go around the back to get to it. There was a stack washer and dryer unit along with a tool chest and a large chest freezer. The door had been locked but opened with the same key that opened the front door. "We are definitely equipped for food that should last us the while we are here," Sarah Ann said with relief. "We will need to somehow repay him for everything we take."

Allen thought for a moment and then asked, "Could we write down everything we take from the freezers and keep track that way?"

"Sounds like a good idea. I'll get a list going, and we will need to remember to write the things down as we use them.

Sarah Ann immediately put some clothes into the washer part of the unit and closing the lid found she couldn't get it going.

Allen discovered that the water leading to the washer

had been turned off for the winter, and after opening the faucet she soon had her first load of laundry finished and in the dryer, and another load in the washer.

The fireplace was doing its job of heating the cabin, and the cold chill soon was gone from the room. There was a small microwave, and Sarah Ann had defrosted enough items so they could cook something for dinner that evening.

Stacked along the wall area beside the laundry room was cut firewood piled to the eaves in four rows that Allen estimated was at least two cords.

The full freezers and all the firewood made Mr. Dolan look like someone who prepared for the worst. "He was prepared for an apocalypse by the look of things," he thought.

They walked out back to the lake and stood there looking around. A couple of cabins could be seen across the lake, but no smoke rose from the chimneys so they took for granted they must be empty. The whole area had a sense of quiet, almost abandonment where it all lay waiting to wake up once again when springtime made its way back from a long cold winter.

The view was beautiful and though the weather was a bit dreary they both agreed that in the summer it must be spectacular. The lake looked to be about a half mile wide and extended away in each direction to what looked about twice that distance. Allen guessed the lake to be somewhere from one and a half to two miles long. It was a nice size and one that you automatically knew had to be well stocked with fish. It wasn't difficult to imagine small boats drifting about and fishermen standing along the shoreline.

Going back inside Sarah Ann stated she was tired and felt like lying down for a while to rest before preparing dinner. "You lie down for as long as you like, I'll make dinner," Allen told her solicitously.

She smiled tiredly and thanked him, making her way to the bedroom where she earlier had prepared the bed with sheets she'd found in a cabinet and fluffed them in the dryer.

Allen began preparing dinner and fried each of them a chicken breast, heating up some frozen corn and digging in the freezer part of the refrigerator found a frozen bag of peaches. He defrosted them and when they were thawed added some sugar. It wasn't the fanciest meal but it would do.

He woke Sarah Ann, and she came to the table, exclaiming over the dinner he had prepared. He'd found several candles in a cabinet above the refrigerator and they ate in the candlelight. It was a scene from a magazine. The fireplace crackling and candlelight glowing on their faces. The only other light was the one above the range shining down from the hood. It was a moment they both instinctively knew they'd look back on for the rest of their lives and they treasured each moment together. They had both experienced life that threatened at keeping them apart and taking each other for granted was something that they never wanted to happen in their lives.

After cleaning up the dishes, they moved to the living room where they snuggled on the sofa, and Allen delighted in feeling life kicking against his hand as he rested it on her stomach.

Mr. Dolan had found them the information they had sought and paid for.

Her mother had two other children, both boys and of high school age. Sarah Ann tingled at knowing she had two half siblings. She had married at the age of 22, almost exactly five years after giving up Sarah Ann. She had met him in college, and they'd married immediately upon her graduation. Sarah Ann had no way of knowing if Lenore had shared the knowledge of having another child with her immediate family, or if it was something she carried in silence.

They finished the evening with a cup of tea and went to bed and both slept soundly.

The silence around the cabin was like nothing they'd experienced in a long while. Finally they weren't wakened to the sounds of closing car doors or noisy people from other rooms.

They woke refreshed and Sarah Ann suggested they go to the store and meet Alice Greenway and pick up a few things they needed while there."I'll make us some omelets and toast when we get back," she said. "Sounds like a plan, but let's not stay too long because I'm hungry."

They left and backtracked to the general store. As they opened the door and entered, a bell hanging on the door jingled. Since they had driven by yesterday, a kind of sad looking Christmas wreath had been hung on the door. However, the interior of the store was much nicer than the outside indicated. The shelves were not as fully stocked, which made sense considering it wasn't a busy time of year. It did however, have milk, eggs and cheese along with some prepackaged lunch meats and a few dismal ready-made sandwiches, the lettuce along the edges sadly wilted in the coolers along the back wall. They picked out what they'd need along with bread and butter and a few other snacks, and rang the buzzer sitting on the counter. It had a small crudely written sign in black marker that pointed to it with the words "Press Here for Service." They heard a female voice call out, "Be right there!" coming from a door somewhere behind the counter. They heard footsteps and then a lady appeared. She was a pleasant looking woman in her mid-sixties.

Chapter 18

S he had hair that was obviously done with a home perm, Sarah Ann guessed.

She was generously proportioned, giving her the grandmotherly look that made it easy to imagine her as someone who children gravitated towards. "Mrs. Greenway?" Allen asked.

She nodded and her smile widened. "Are you the Gingerich's?" They told her yes, and she proceeded to tell them she'd been expecting them. "So things are going well with you?" She gestured toward Sarah Ann's distended stomach.

"Yes, besides having a sore back and being tired, I feel well. But I suppose that's to be expected." "It definitely is," she agreed and then said with a proud smile added, "I had five myself and delivered four of my seven grandchildren."

"Mr. Dolan told us that you may be able to help us with the delivery," Sarah Ann said hopefully. "I would be pleased to, it's been a couple of years but I still remember how quite well."

They moved on to other subjects, and she didn't pry. "Fred told me that you have some things you are working through and I am here to help, not get in your business," she told them kindly.

Allen and Sarah Ann thanked her and left.

Sarah Ann made good on her promise, and soon they were seated eating delicious omelets, toast and sipping orange juice.

*****

..........She sat in her office, her wall holding several plaques showing off her successes. She knew that what the wall proclaimed about her was not what she felt much of the time. Her life had become one where joy didn't seem to find its way in much anymore. Her husband was gone abroad once again for a month, and somewhere in the past six years the closeness that once existed between them had dissipated. To the point where it seemed more like two people sharing a home as roommates, than ones who had known what it meant to have been passionately in love in some prior life. And though she suspected infidelities on his part to the point where suspecting no longer seemed to need proof, she also knew that her own life had enough secrets to not feel too judgmental about his. It was, after all, her own guilt that had eventually grown to where she pushed him from the closeness they had once shared.

She sighed as she looked at the photo of her two sons that sat on her desk. The picture was taken about six months prior on a rare family vacation spent at the beach. It was taken while walking on the boardwalk on the way to a local seafood place that was boasted to be amazing. It was a rare moment she had captured and she treasured it. They had stopped, and both were standing looking out across the water like they were posing. Nicolas, the eldest was leaning on the railing of the boardwalk, and Alexander was standing erect with his hand placed on his shoulder. When the boys saw the photo later, Alexander had claimed his hand was caught poking his brother to point out what he thought may have been dolphins in the water. She had, however, loved the picture and marveled at the perfect moment she had managed to capture. If only the rest of her life was that perfect. She was proud of her sons. Both were accomplished at what they liked to do and they had always gotten along. They were two years apart in age and though they had competitive moments growing up, both had always been each other's best friend.

Her life probably appeared great to those looking in, but she and her husband knew the truth.

So far she had been able to keep up appearances with the boys and she fought to hang on until at least when they were both out of school and in college.

Her phone buzzed, and she picked it up. "Mrs. Collins, your three o clock appointment is here. Shall I send him in?" her friendly assistant Betsy asked. "Give me thirty seconds," she replied. Mentally pulling herself together, she got ready for another hour long session with someone she sometimes felt like shaking rather than listening to.

At times, it seemed a bit strange when she listened to others and all their issues, that she could have told them, "If they thought they had problems, let her spill hers." But she kept silent and went on day after day living with a secret that time had not helped to erase. When her day finally ended, she drove home in her new Mercedes S63. It was a present that Jonathan had gotten for her, and she drove it simply because it fit her image.

She unlocked the door and stepped inside of her 5,600

Summer vacation was winding down and only one week remained. They had all agreed to make the most out of the time left. When they finally had enough of jumping in the water, they made their way back to Lance's back patio where they sat drinking root beer floats and joking around in the carefree way that only teens seem to be able to do. Finally, as everyone was leaving, Lance had grabbed her arm and said in a low voice, "Don't leave, Lennie."

So she had stayed and even though she knew the temptations that existed, she somehow fooled herself into believing she was stronger. She would not give in and be like so many of the other girls she'd found herself scoffing about. The ones who became pregnant and ruined their lives.

But when she knew with certainty about a month later that she was pregnant, she found out then the harsh judgments that people can make with very little understanding.

She knew if her own mother had been living that her circumstances would certainly have been different. Her father had grown into an uncaring man who really didn't pay enough attention to her anymore to even care who she spent her time with or in what they would be doing.

Her responsibilities included the laundry, and if she had a warm meal for him at the end of his day it was enough to keep him out of her affairs. She had learned the hard way, when in her negligence, he was without clean socks except for several singles he had to pair together that were definitely no match. He didn't lay his hands on her, but the tone and harshness of his voice as he scolded her were just as painful as any physical pain he could have inflicted.

She had never allowed herself to search for her daughter, choosing to believe that if fate intended she would somehow make her way back to her.

The decision to give up the baby wasn't really as difficult as others may have imagined. She didn't want a baby growing up in a home with her father as the head of the home. She had too often heard his comments of how Lenore was like her mother, and it was never the complimentary things he was mentioning. Raising a child took money and she had none.

The school counselor had given her a few brochures on choices of what she could do, and she knew right away that an abortion wasn't something she wanted to do.

So she had chosen an adoption agency, one that spoke glowingly of homes where babies were taken in and loved and cherished as their own. The pretty young woman she had spoken to had even offered to be with her as she delivered. She had taken her up on the offer, as she had no one else. She was told that she had a choice of whether or not to hold the baby after the delivery.

She had chosen to hold her, marveling at the beautiful little being she had helped create.

If she had not known that some other woman would take her and love her as her own mother had loved her, she would have run from the room screaming, chasing after them as they walked down the hallway and taking the baby from her forever. But she had that to give her solace, and though over the next months her arms felt so empty, she clung to the knowledge that little Julia was happy and well cared for.

She had set the timer on her cell phone and it was indicating that it was time for her to get out and go rescue the casserole.

She entered the kitchen again seeing the red glow on the answering machine. It was no longer blinking but she couldn't forget the message that remained.

She took the casserole out of the oven, placing it on a hot plate on the counter. Going over to the answering machine, she once again clicked the play button and listened to the message replay.

Something made her write the number down and she had to press play for the third time so she could get all the numbers. She had the next morning off of work as there was a long overdue dental appointment, and she thought maybe then she'd call and find out who this Sarah Ann was.

The door leading in from the garage opened, and her boys came in, boisterously talking as they bantered about some plays in basketball. She turned to them, putting a smile into place as she greeted them and told them she'd have their plates ready in a moment.

Momentarily, she was able to push aside her pain as she sat with her sons and listened to their day.

Chapter 19

As Sarah Ann hung up the phone, she wondered if she shouldn't have left a message but rather just called back later. She'd give her until the next afternoon and then try again. Allen was carrying more wood in for the fire, and when he finished she told him about the call. He tried to encourage her by telling her that Lenore may very well be calling her back.

Sarah Ann had not really rehearsed that much in her mind as to what she'd be saying to Lenore if she did call her back.

The answering machine message had identified itself as being the Collins residence, so she was sure that it had been the correct number they had been given.

She pushed her disappointment aside and concentrated on preparing a good dinner for Allen.

Earlier, he had discovered a rack full of books in the loft, so they had both chosen several that looked interesting and Sarah was well into one that she was fully enjoying.

She knew that being Amish was made easier by her love for reading. Having grown up with a television and radio, she had found at times that she missed them, but having books helped her through those times. Even now thinking of a day when the danger would set them free from needing to hide, she couldn't really imagine a life apart from the Amish. It was what she knew Allen wanted and she had grown to love his parents and she hoped that someday they could go back to their life before her accident.

She dished out the food and told Allen it was ready to eat. They sat down at the table and in Amish fashion bowed their heads in silent prayer.

*****

"How about a walk?" Allen suggested the next morning.

"Sure, I feel up to it. Other than feeling as big as a house I feel good enough for a walk. The exercise would do me good as well."

She bundled herself in a coat and they went out in the cold crisp air. There had been a hard frost and though it hadn't snowed, it didn't seem difficult to imagine that soon it would. "Does it snow much in Missouri?" she asked Allen.

"It does at times but not nearly the amount that we get in Michigan, but that's due to getting a lot of lake-effect snow."

"I like Missouri," Sarah Ann said. "It's really pretty here. I like the hills."

"So do I. They also have Amish churches here in Missouri."

"They do? I didn't know that! Are we close to them now?"

"I really don't know exactly how near we are to them, but when we get back to the cabin, I'll look at the atlas and see."

They had walked out the driveway and headed up the

road in the opposite direction than the general store. Sarah Ann knew she had better not overdo the walking, but she was having such an enjoyable time she regretted needing to turn around. But Allen insisted so they started back.

They returned and took off their coats. Allen was heating water for tea, and Sarah Ann had settled on the sofa when the phone rang.

It was Alice Greenway just checking on them making sure everything was fine. They assured her they were doing well and finally after the kettle started whistling she said good bye.

Allen carried the cups to the sofa and they sat staring in the flames. "Have you ever regretted marrying me?" Sarah Ann suddenly asked. "Depends on what you mean by regretting."

"Your life with me has not been anywhere near what a normal Amish marriage should be, and I wonder if you have regretted marrying me."

"Maybe I wasn't looking for a typical Amish life. And the answer to your question is no, I have not regretted marrying you." Allen paused and then continued, "That doesn't mean that I haven't wished circumstances weren't like they are. But that's not regretting marrying you."

"I told myself that you didn't regret it or else you'd not have come after me, but I had to hear it from you." Sarah Ann told him with a look of relief on her face.

Allen leaned over and kissed her gently on the side of her mouth. "Please don't ever question my love for you again. Now where is that atlas, let's see how far the Amish are from here."

Allen went to the car for the atlas and when he came back found Missouri. "I remember reading in the Budget there's about 5,000 Amish in Missouri. I remember a few of the towns but not many." "That many Amish?" Sarah Ann exclaimed, "I had no idea there would be that many in Missouri."

Allen found that the nearest Amish to them would be in Seymour.

He explained that among all the different sects of Amish, they were one of the strictest.

Sarah Ann declared that it would not be the one she'd want to live in were they to ever move to Missouri.

They had just finished their cups of tea when the phone rang once again. Something tightened inside Sarah Ann and she instinctively felt it was Lenore returning her call.

She motioned to Allen to remain sitting and lumbered to her feet. Going to the table she picked up the phone. Taking a deep breath she clicked "send" to connect and said, "Hello?"

"Is this Sarah Ann Gingerich," a female voice inquired. Sarah Ann guessed it to be fortyish sounding. It was a pleasant modulated tone. Sarah Ann thought it would sound good in a recording, and wondered with such a voice why they had a computer recording on their message machine and not just use this voice.

"Yes, this is Sarah Ann Gingerich," she affirmed. "This is Lenore Collins, you left a message asking me to call." She said it as more of a question than a statement. "Yes, ah..." Sarah Ann hesitated for a moment, searching for the words, "I know this may come as a shock to you, and I don't know how else to say this but just say it. I was given up for adoption when I was a baby, and I am fairly certain you may be my mother." She sat down at the table. Her heart pounded, as she heard silence at the other end of the line. She waited as the seconds ticked by.

*****

Lenore sat down heavily on the edge of her bed. Her mouth was open in shock. So many years had passed, and she had spent each one waiting eagerly for this moment to come and now that it had she sat dumbfounded with no words.

"Hello?" she heard Sarah Ann say hesitantly. "If I've called the wrong person, I am so sorry."

"No, you haven't. At least I don't believe you have," she finally managed to say. "When is your birthday?"

Sarah Ann told her the day and certainty overcame her that this was indeed her little baby she had given up so long ago. She quivered inside, excitement overcoming her. "There are so many things I'd like to ask you," she said. "First, where are you now?"

"I am currently in Missouri, but it's a long story." "I am in North Carolina. I'd love to meet you."

"I'd love to meet you too," Sarah Ann said. "I really didn't know I was adopted until four years ago."

"There's so many things I have been dying to know about you and asking over the phone just doesn't seem right – may I come see you?" Lenore asked and then wondered if maybe she was being too eager. She may just frighten her away if she wasn't careful. "I'd really like that." I am married, and we are having our first child very soon."

"Oh my, how exciting!" Lenore exclaimed. "Yes, it is. Do you really want to come see me and meet us?"

Lenore hesitated. "Sarah Ann, this is the first time in 23 years that I can tell an ache inside me is gone. Coming to see you would be the most amazing thing in the world."

"My husband's name is Allen; you will like him a lot." Sarah Ann told her with pride in her voice. "Here, I will put him on the phone so he can say hello to you as well."

"I am sure I shall like him very much," Lenore agreed with a smile.

Sarah Ann handed the phone to Allen, and he greeted his new mother-in-law. He spoke to Lenore for a few minutes and then handed the phone back to his wife. "He is a very nice young man," Lenore said with fervor in her voice.

They talked for a while longer, and Lenore hung up the phone.

She sat in almost a stupor. Rising she made her way to the bathroom and stood at her side of the double sinks. She looked different somehow and she recognized what it was. It had been so long since she'd seen or felt it, but she knew with certainty that what she was seeing in her eyes was joy.

She clasped her hands to her chest, breathing in excitedly. She was going to meet Julia. No, she corrected herself in her mind, Sarah Ann. She liked the name, and she definitely liked the young woman she had spoken to. Her husband had sounded kind as well and she knew no matter what difficulty may stand in her path, nothing was going to prevent her from meeting her daughter.

*****

Sarah Ann grasped her stomach as a sharp pain stabbed her and made her wince.

Allen leaned forward, "Are you okay?" he asked anxiously.

She smiled at his concern. "It really hurts, but I suspect I'll survive."

"Do you think I should call Mrs. Greenway and ask her to stop by and see how things are going?" Allen asked.

Sarah Ann nodded, "It can't hurt to know how much longer."

Allen rose and walked to the kitchen counter where he'd placed the phone after the call with Lenore.

Mrs. Greenway answered on the third ring and agreed to come over soon as she could put a closed sign up and put in a new load of laundry. "I do laundry on the side for extra income," she explained to Allen. "Every little bit helps."

She arrived about 20 minutes later, bustling in and taking immediate charge. Allen and Sarah Ann both felt grateful for her motherly concern as she carefully examined Sarah Ann. "It'll be more than just a few more hours," she confidently informed them.

"That's not the news we were hoping to hear." Sarah Ann groaned a little and tried to laugh but ended it abruptly when her laugh was cut short by a sharp stab of pain. "Basically, try to stay as calm and rested as you can, Sarah Ann," she instructed in a firm voice.

There isn't much I can do now but I'll stop back in a few hours. Now I'm getting back to my laundry."

Allen noticed the wood needed to be replenished and got up to go get more. He first made sure Sarah Ann didn't need anything before he went out into the cold.

A light snow had begun to fall, and Allen could tell by the clouds in the air that a lot more snow could be falling before long.

He stood gazing across the lake, feeling a sudden ache of homesickness for his parents and home. He missed the life he had there. Now that Sarah Ann was alive and his short stint teaching school was over he wanted nothing more than to be able to go back to life like it was a year ago.

But first there were matters that needed to be taken care of and standing here wishing for something else wouldn't help a baby be born. Allen gathered a large armful and headed for the door, noticing how the snow was beginning to come down with more intensity. It was mid-afternoon and still a few more hours of daylight remained. Allen decided he'd see how the weather was when dark came or he'd see about maybe taking Sarah Ann to Mrs. Greenway's house. That way come what may weather-wise, they would at least be in her capable hands.

Preparing some tea, he carried a cup to the bedroom where Sarah Ann lay resting. She had her eyes closed but he could see her lids flicker as another contraction came over her.

He placed the cup on the nightstand, gently stroking her cheek. She opened her eyes and looked up at him and smiled. Clasping his hand with her own she said, "Please lay down beside me."

"I brought you some tea, but it needs to cool down a little anyway." He lay beside her and propped himself up on his elbow, looking down at her. He loved everything about her face.

He was still in amazement that this beautiful woman loved him as much as he loved her.

She sighed and looking at him she said in a rather sad voice. "I'm so glad that Lenore is going to be in my life, but there's still so many things I have to sort through about how I feel about Malinda." She gave a half sob and went on, "I was laying here and thinking back over my life, especially my younger years and I can honestly say I loved them. They seemed like parents to me. But now since talking to Lenore, I am feeling guilt and I don't understand why."

Allen thought it over for a bit, cautious to speak too suddenly. He had read in a book on relationships too often in a marriage that a husband will try to fix a problem, without understanding his wife just wanted to be heard and feel comforted.

"That makes sense to me." he finally said. "She felt like your mother all those years and why wouldn't it seem like betrayal to suddenly declare otherwise. But you have to remember your circumstances are a bit different than if she really had been your mother. They kept the truth from you all those years and no matter what the reasons may have been, they shouldn't have you feeling any guilt over now having a relationship with Lenore."

She smiled tremulously, big tears shining from the corners of her eyes. Pushing herself up, she shoved a pillow behind her back and said, "Now where is that tea?"

He laughed and handed her the cup, cautioning her to be careful.

"I love you Allen, thank you for always being so patient and kind."

He teasingly said, "You are very welcome, but you forgot 'wise.'"

She laughingly punched his arm and then stopped and breathed as another pain engulfed her. "I'm so glad we have this nice cabin to be in. I feel so safe here." Sarah Ann said gratefully after it had subsided. "Praise God for Mr. Dolan and his caring heart," Allen agreed.

Chapter 20

Allen rose and went to the living room to check on the fire. Adding a few chunks of wood to the blaze, he stood at the kitchen window looking out. The snow had not slowed, but if anything had increased in volume. The wind picking up as well and Allen could see small areas where the snow was being blown from the ground. He remembered hearing that babies are born at most inopportune times and had to agree this could be counted as one of those.

Mrs. Greenway came driving up just then, snow billowing out from behind her as she drove in the driveway.

Allen opened the door for her and she greeted him enthusiastically, stomping her feet free of snow before entering. "How's Sarah Ann doing?" she asked midway on her way to the bedroom.

A few minutes later, she announced happily, "It's getting closer time. Still be several more hours though. Hard telling how this weather is going to be like and I really don't want to have to go back out in this later. Why don't both of you just pack up and come on over to my house?"

Allen saw the wisdom in the suggestion and Sarah Ann also readily agreed. "Go on ahead and we'll be right over," Allen told her and she nodded her permed head.

Placing her hand knitted stocking cap back on her head, she said she'd be prepared for them and left.

Allen told Sarah Ann there was no need to hurry that they still had an hour of daylight. They gathered what they would need and Allen carefully helped Sarah Ann to the car.

They had both heard of people who hoard and are called hoarders, but they were not prepared for the condition of Alice Greenway's home. Boxes were piled along the walls from floor to ceiling. Rows of them made up narrow paths for them to walk through. She led them through several of the paths to a bedroom that was surprisingly empty compared to the rest of what they'd already seen. A four-poster bed with a canopy dominated the room along with a nightstand and dresser.

An old cedar chest was placed at the foot end of the bed. It had a pretty crocheted afghan laying across the top.

Picking up the afghan, Mrs. Greenway lay it on the bed. "Here you go dear; if you get cold, wrap yourself in this," she kindly told Sarah Ann. "I crocheted that thing years ago.

Allen felt butterflies in his stomach now that the time was so near to deliver the baby. What exactly did the father do in the situation? Growing up Amish it wasn't a customary thing for men to talk about and he felt rather helpless. "Is it true that you boil water?" he asked Mrs. Greenway.

She chuckled a little bit and said, "I think the main intent of that was to give the father's something to do more than anything. Back in the old days when that saying was made popular, water had to be drawn from a well, a fire had to be built to boil the water. It took quite a bit of time, and kept the man preoccupied."

Sarah Ann touched his hand. "You can talk to me and help me through it. That will help more than anything."

Mrs. Greenway left them alone after telling them to holler if they needed her.

"I wonder what's in all those boxes." Allen wondered aloud.

"I thought the same thing." Sarah Ann admitted. "It surely can't all be merchandise for the store."

An hour slowly dragged by, and finally Sarah Ann felt like she couldn't bear much more. "Can you please call her?" She panted the request.

Allen backtracked his way through the paths he'd taken earlier and called Mrs. Greenway's name. He heard her reply from another room and told her what he wanted.

"I'll be right there," she promised, and he returned to Sarah Ann.

The birth was one of the most horrendous things Allen had ever witnessed. He'd seen a calf being born before but this didn't seem anything remotely the same. He would look back later and gratefully realize the miracle of birth outweighed the horror.

It seemed forever until a baby's cry pierced the air, and when a little boy was laid in his arms he had never felt so proud in his life. It wasn't long before Sarah Ann began experiencing more birth pains and suddenly Mrs. Greenway realized she was about to have twins. A short while later, a little girl made her entry into the world and with a gusty cry made her presence known.

A few minutes later Sarah Ann lay with two babies snuggled in her arms, tired but very happy.

"Do you have names chosen for them?" asked Mrs. Greenway.

"I had a girl name chosen." Sarah Ann replied. "For some reason I sensed it would be a little girl. I like Lena Rose, named after my oldest and dearest friend."

"I like Lawrence," Allen suddenly said. "Lena Rose and Lawrence, what do you think?"

Sarah Ann thought for a moment and smiled. "I don't mind at all, Lawrence it shall be."

"You should rest now." Mrs. Greenway strongly suggested to Sarah Ann. She told Allen there was a bassinet that would be large enough for both babies. "I couldn't carry it by myself or else I'd have had it in here for you." She sounded apologetic.

Allen followed her to another room and rolled the bassinet slowly back to the babies. It barely fit through in some places. The boxes stacked like fortress walls around him. "Do you know what is in all these boxes?" he asked and then felt maybe he'd been rude by asking.

She laughed. "Lots of them I don't. I know most of the items I have but I couldn't tell you which boxes they were in."

They put the bassinet in the corner and Mrs. Greenway placed freshly laundered bedding inside.

Allen held little Lena Rose in his arms, and he was in wonder as he looked at her tiny perfect features. Her little fingers clutched the edge of the blanket, and her mouth opened in a yawn.

He put his head near hers and whispered softly, "I

promise to do my best to keep you safe and provide you with the best home possible." He looked up with tears in his eyes and found Sarah Ann watching him, her own eyes brimming. Everything they had been through the past several weeks catching up to them.

Allen felt exhausted, and he could hardly imagine how Sarah Ann must be feeling.

He gently lay the baby in the bassinet and watched them both sleeping, so unaware of anything around them. Sarah Ann said she needed to use the bathroom, and he helped her out of bed.

She returned and asked, "Allen, did you remember to bring our toothbrushes and toothpaste?"

He remembered that he hadn't and there was a bag of baby items they'd forgotten as well.

Allen said he'd quickly run back to the cabin to get the items.

The cabin was only a half mile walk, and he didn't want to disturb Alice by opening the creaky garage door so decided to walk the short distance and stepped outside. Only a few flakes still floated in the moonlight.

The air was crisp and clear, and he took a deep breath filling his lungs.

He thought of his parents and hoped the neighbors had kept their promise to deliver the news of the safe delivery of the twins.

Amanda especially would be thrilled, and he couldn't wait to show them off.

The snow crunched under his feet as he tried to walk inside a tire track from a vehicle that had passed through earlier.

The magnitude of the future ahead for them loomed, and he prayed that somehow circumstances would change and they could live a life free of worry and harm.

He was willing to dedicate a lifetime to protecting his family and keeping them safe, though.

He passed the stump and turned onto the driveway. The tire tracks from when they'd left that morning had all but disappeared from all the snow.

Seeming like a very long time since they'd left but it really had been only half a day. The cabin loomed in the moonlight, and he unlocked the door and went in.

The fireplace lay cold and dark, the fire long dead.

Allen made his way to the bedroom, realizing he'd forgotten to turn the light on.

Growing up Amish had him lighting lamps, and he wasn't yet accustomed to the convenience of flipping a switch on the wall.

He did however turn on the light in the bedroom and immediately saw the bag Sarah Ann had mentioned. Picking it up, he went to the bathroom next to the bedroom to get the few toiletry items they had forgotten. He'd just turned off the light and was making his way back to the front door when he heard an engine sound and heard a vehicle coming up the driveway.

It only had parking lights on, and something about the vehicle told him it wasn't someone coming to wish him well.

Chapter 21

He cast around in his mind what he should do and quickly climbed the ladder to the loft. It had a window that looked out over the small lean-to where Sarah Ann had done the laundry with about a four-foot drop to the roof below.

He quickly unlocked and opened the window. Barely fitting through the opening he pushed himself through and dropped down. He had to stretch to reach but was able to pull the window back down.

Hoping they hadn't heard him he lay on his side flattened against the wall of the cabin.

He was safe from being seen unless they opened the window and put their head outside to look down.

He heard voices and heard the crunching of the snow as they walked around the building.

"They were definitely here; a few of the ashes are still a little warm," he heard one of them say.

Allen wondered how many there were. Two were outside, and he thought he heard someone in the loft, so that made three.

When the opportunity came, he was going to make a run for it. He mentally prepared himself for the drop off the lean-to then thought of which direction would be best to run. Behind the cabin lay the lake, and he didn't want to lead them toward Sarah Ann and the babies. That only left the driveway or into the woods and, he chose the latter.

He hoped they'd leave soon now that they hadn't found them.

His side was beginning to get numb from laying in the same position, and the cold had seeped through the fabric. He gently shifted a little to keep the blood flowing and felt some snow fall into his collar. The crunching noise from feet sounded, and he again heard them talk as they made their way past.

"We should just stay for the night," one of them said. "There's plenty of wood and food."

"Let's do it," the other agreed. The voices faded as they went around the front of the building.

Allen knew he'd have to make a move soon. He was getting cold and wanted his reflexes to work properly.

He waited a while longer until he thought everything was quiet, and they were settled.

His shoulder was numb from the cold, and he hoped his leg wouldn't give out on him when he dropped from the roof. He slowly moved toward the edge and away from the window.

Finally, he was able to peer over the side.

The quietness of the night mocked the severity of the situation.

He saw nothing and waited a moment longer then slowly lowered his body over the side.

He had extended himself fully and was hanging on by the tips of his fingers ready to drop the few feet to the ground when he suddenly heard the door open.

They were coming to get more wood for the fireplace,

and he had nowhere to hide.

Making the decision to drop and run, he let go and hit the ground. His leg caved a little, and he crashed awkwardly into the wall before gaining his balance and taking off at a speed fueled by fear. He felt something tug at his sleeve at the same time he heard a bark of gunfire.

The shock of realizing he'd so narrowly been missed kept him running, and he weaved a little so he'd become a more difficult target. Entering the woods, he jumped over a fallen log and continued running.

He was praying frantically in his mind as he ran through the brambles, and they finally stopped shooting.

They must have run out of bullets, he decided. He could hear the third one yelling from the cabin.

Allen afforded himself a quick look over his shoulder and saw he was being followed.

One of the men was as swift as Allen, and he wasn't breaking stride.

Allen's lungs felt like they would burst, but he forced himself on.

Allen was grateful for the adequate light that showed enough of the way that allowed him to not run into bushes and branches.

Just in time, he managed to see a deep gully that looked to drop off to a depth he didn't have the time to look into. He veered sharply to the left and ran alongside the deep ravine.

It led him in the direction of the road and he knew that he'd made the right decision since the other way led to the lake.

It allowed his pursuer to gain a few steps on him as he

quickly turned before reaching the point where Allen had turned.

Allen guessed the road had to lay within 500 feet ahead of him, and he saw the headlights of the vehicle as the driver tore out of the driveway. He quickly calculated they'd probably reach the same spot on the road at the same time.

Cutting a sharp left, he made his way back toward the driveway and saw the vehicle passing by on the road. Slamming on the brakes, the SUV backed up and quickly turned around.

Allen reached the driveway and stopped when a man suddenly loomed in front of him.

"Stop or I'll blow your head off," the man said in a no-nonsense tone.

Allen didn't doubt him one bit and stopped. He stood there breathing heavily

The man called out to the others,

"I've got him!"

Allen's pursuer came up just then and stood there. He was hardly panting, and Allen realized that it would only have been a matter of time before he'd been run into the ground. The man was way too accustomed to running to have allowed Allen to get away from him.

The SUV came up the driveway and followed them as they walked the short distance up the driveway and to the cabin. A gun poked against Allen's back, and he knew that there was no way he was going to chance whether it was out of bullets.

In the cabin, he was shoved roughly onto the kitchen chair. One of them held the gun on him while another went to the vehicle for rope.

The one tying him showed no mercy as he jerked the rope tight around his wrists and the chest, strapping him tightly to the back of the chair.

He thought two of them looked familiar and tried desperately to remember where he'd seen them before. It suddenly dawned on him they were the men sitting in the vehicle outside the supermarket that day he'd driven to town with Amos.

The third one, who had been driving the SUV down the road, came inside just then. He appeared to be the leader and stepped up authoritatively to Allen and began to question him.

He wore rectangular rimless glasses and had light gray eyes. They were set a little close together and gave him a hungry, wolfish appearance. Allen felt himself quake at the coldness he saw in his eyes.

"You're going to tell me where she is, Amish boy," he said.

One of the other men snickered and glanced toward Allen with an aggravated look.

Allen didn't say anything. He wasn't sure he could even if told to. Nothing he'd ever read in any of the books had prepared him for a time like this.

The man reached out and smacked him sharply across the cheek. "I'm talking to you!"

Allen's head jerked, his cheek stinging. He felt sudden rage as the fear subsided and the realization of what the men wanted from him sank in.

"I won't tell you where she is," he declared with a deep conviction.

"Then we'll have to make you tell us," the man said. His gray eyes gleamed as if the thought seemed to fill him with excitement.

Allen didn't doubt the man would enjoy whatever form of torture they'd use to get him to speak.

"Why are you doing this?" Allen asked, hoping maybe he could stall them.

"It doesn't matter why. It only matters that you tell us what we want to know."

"Sarah Ann is a good person. She deserves to live."

"Good person or not, I only do what I am told to do," the man said with little care.

He walked over to the fireplace and picked up the poker that stood leaning against the brick.

"See this boy? I am going to make this red hot and then we'll see if you'll talk or not."

Allen shuddered at the thought of what a hot poker could do but tried to pretend stoic and not show how frightened he was.

The other two men were rummaging carelessly through the cabinets and refrigerator.

Finding a couple of canned soups in the cabinet, they managed to find the can opener and heated the soup in the small microwave. Pouring it into bowls they sat at the table and began eating greedily like they hadn't eaten in a while.

They slurped each bite until the leader finally yelled at them.

"Stop eating like pigs!" he told them disgustedly. "Seriously, I only keep you two clowns around because I need you."

Allen tried to not think of the poker that lay in the burning coals.

He knew it would take the heat of a torch to make it glow, but it would still be hot enough to inflict some serious injury and pain.

Desperately he tried to think of something to say that may possibly change their minds but knew it was hopeless. His only avenue of escape would be a prayer for a miracle.

Too much time, effort and money had been spent on searching for them, and they were sure to finish what they'd set out to do.

"What are your names?" Allen asked, trying to break the awkward silence.

They ignored him and continued eating as if he didn't exist.

The leader sat on the sofa idly paging through a hunting magazine Allen had been reading earlier that morning.

Allen closed his eyes and prayed, asking God to grant him the strength to remain strong.

Come what may he could not put Sarah Ann and the babies in danger by revealing their whereabouts.

He still had his head bowed when he heard the man rise from the sofa.

Chapter 22

Allen couldn't help but watch as the man pulled the hot poker from the flames. A tendril of black smoke drifted upward from the tip.

He moved toward Allen, holding it up and showing it to him. His eyes gleamed with a wolfish glow, and he was almost salivating as the thought of torture seemed to fill him with desire.

"I'm going to ask you just once more. Where is she?" He grabbed Allen by the hair jerking him back a little. Allen struggled a little but the ropes around his chest kept him from being able to move.

Suddenly, there was a sound at the door, and it crashed open. A man came rushing in, his gun drawn, and he began shooting. The leader quickly reached for his gun but fell back as a bullet buried itself into his stomach. The men around the table both tried hitting the floor, but one wasn't quite fast enough.

Allen tried to register what was happening, but it had all transpired so quickly. He'd just managed to get it through his mind that it was Mr. Dolan when the man shot from under the table. The bullet hit Mr. Dolan in the upper thigh, and his leg buckled as he fell and dropped his gun to the floor.

Allen saw the leader's gun laying by his foot and quickly kicked it to Mr. Dolan. Grabbing it with his hand, in one smooth move he quickly cocked and fired it the moment he had it raised.

Allen could tell he was no novice when it came to handling and shooting firearms.

Blood was flowing in a steady flow from the bullet wound in Mr. Dolan's leg when he managed to stand. He hobbled over to the two men and made sure they wouldn't be moving before coming over to Allen. He lay the gun on the table near Allen and untied him as quickly as he could.

"I called 911 a while ago," Dolan said grimacing in pain. "They should be here soon."

"What made you come here?" Allen asked curiously. "How did you know to come?"

"After those guys left, I just couldn't rest easy. I knew they were bad news, and I couldn't just leave you and Sarah Ann to fend for yourselves. I thought I'd come up here and see how things were going for you." He sat down heavily in the kitchen chair, keeping the gun ready in case any of them made a sudden move. "When I called Alice Greenway, she told me you'd be staying at her house overnight. So I thought I'd save myself the hotel bill by sleeping here. I had stopped at her house and was walking out to my car when I heard the gunshots. Figured they were up to no good, so I hiked it here fast as I could.

I waited outside for as long as I could for the cops to get here, but when I saw him with the hot poker I had to make my move."

Allen was in amazement. God had answered his prayer in such a miraculous way. Once again Mr. Dolan had appeared like an unlikely angel to the rescue.

"I don't even know how to thank you," he said gratefully. "Words can't express how much I appreciate all you've done."

"Can you please grab a bath towel and wrap it around my leg?" Mr. Dolan instructed.

Allen raced to the bathroom and quickly grabbed a clean white towel. He tied it tightly around Mr. Dolan's leg to staunch the flow of blood.

There was a knock and a call at the door and officers began entering the room.

"We have paramedics on the way," one of them explained.

The leader was still alive, and the shot to his gut caused him to moan in pain. One of the other men had been shot through the head, and the third suffered a wound to the chest that just missed his heart.

Allen was glad they weren't able to hurt anyone anymore but was glad they hadn't died.

The paramedics finally arrived and quickly administered first aid to Mr. Dolan and the two men.

Allen promised to come to the hospital the next day to see Mr. Dolan. He wished him a speedy recovery, and then a police officer dropped him off at Alice Greenway's home.

Sarah Ann had heard the gunshots and had been frantic waiting to hear what had happened. She'd seen the police cars go past, followed soon after by the ambulances. She fell into Allen's arms when he entered the house. Allen told her and Alice everything that had happened.

"What I can't understand," Sarah Ann said wonderingly, "why has Mr. Dolan done so much for us and so unselfishly?"

Alice looked like she knew the answer and she hesitated. "I guess it would be okay for me to tell you."

She paused for a moment. "The story starts a long time ago. Fred was married to a wonderful lady. They had a son together who they both loved very much. She died from cancer when the boy was about thirteen, and Fred had such difficulty recovering from the loss. He turned to drinking, and the boy was kind of forgotten along the way. When he turned eighteen, he'd been in so much trouble that finally in a last ditch attempt to stay out of jail he joined the military. It was during Desert Storm, and he went off to war. Sadly, he was killed overseas, and he and Fred never really reconciled."

She wiped her eyes as the sadness of the story touched her as well. Allen and Sarah Ann sat listening feeling sadness for the wonderful man they'd learned to know and appreciate. They were wiping tears as well.

"Fred told me that when he first met you Allen, he was struck by how much you looked the same," Alice continued. "Although Allen was older, the resemblance to his son was very striking. He felt that somehow helping you would perhaps help make up for everything he'd not done for his own son."

Allen felt very humbled and all he felt was appreciation and a deep gladness.

He and Sarah Ann both marveled that for now at least they were safe.

After saying good night to Alice, they both went to bed. They were both exhausted.

Allen awoke what seemed just a short while later, the

cry of a baby waking him from a sound sleep.

For a second Allen was confused. Why was a baby crying in their bedroom?

He felt Sarah Ann stir, and not wanting her to get up he quickly told her to stay in bed.

Lawrence was the one crying, and Allen gently gave him to Sarah Ann. His cries stopped immediately when he found the nourishment he was seeking.

"This will be our lives from now on," Sarah Ann said in a tired but happy tone.

"Definitely will be different," Allen agreed, his mind still very clogged by sleep.

Everything was still for a few moments then Sarah Ann broke the quiet. "I want to call Lenore tomorrow and tell her about the twins."

"I want to let my parents know as well. I can call the neighbors and they'll give them the message,"

Allen finished in mid yawn.

Daylight came, and he rose to meet the morning. He didn't feel very rested and shuddered to think of how Sarah Ann must be feeling.

He dressed quietly to not waken Sarah Ann. Making his way to the kitchen, Allen heard humming and found Mrs. Greenway making coffee in an old fashioned percolator. The water was bubbling and the smell of coffee was in the air.

"Good morning, Allen! What does it feel like to be a daddy?"

He smiled back. "So far so good. Mrs. Greenway—"

She cut him off. "Please call me Alice," she said with a cheerful smile.

"Mrs. Gr...er Alice," he said soberly, "I have a favor to ask."

"What is it, Allen?" she reached into the cupboard and pulled out several cups.

"Until everything gets ironed out, we really have no place to stay. Would it be okay for us to stay a while longer?

"Of course, you are welcome to stay here."

"It may be a while before Sarah Ann is able to travel."

"I know, but it's not going to hurt anything to have you around for a few weeks. Besides, I'll enjoy the company." She lifted a cup and taking the handle of the coffee pot. "Would you like a cup?"

He accepted and thanked her for everything.

She poured the coffee into a carafe. "It will be right here if you'd like more later."

Allen thanked her and sat at the table, looking out at the snow. The snow had finally stopped falling during the night, and he guessed there was close to six inches of snow on the ground.

Draining the last few drops in his mouth, he rose and made his way to the sink, where he set his cup gently in the stainless steel bottom.

Alice returned back to the kitchen. "Allen, I will be making Sarah Ann breakfast later. Just let me know when she is feeling hungry."

"I'll let you know."

When he returned, Sarah Ann was holding one of the babies. He guessed it to be Lena Rose.

The babies looked very much alike and without seeing what colors they wore, he had a difficult time telling them apart.

In spite of his concern, he still managed to put on a cheerful face for Sarah Ann.

"I'd really like to call Lenore this morning," Sarah Ann said while turning the baby over against her shoulder and gently patting her back.

"It's Saturday, so she is probably off of work," Allen replied. "Did she mention what she did for a living?"

"I don't believe she told me, but I was so nervous I may not have heard either. I'm afraid that after coming so close to having her in my life that I will lose her before ever meeting her."

"With love comes courage," Allen said with conviction. "I had to make that choice when I left the Amish and everything I had known to find you."

"You've given up so much to be with me," Sarah Ann said gratefully. "And I love you so much for it."

"I don't want you to feel like you owe me or are under any obligation. What I did was my own decision, a choice made out of love for you and I'd do it all over again."

Chapter 23

They spent the morning enjoying the babies. Allen loved holding them, and found the task quite easy to read and hold a baby in his arms at the same time.

Alice had quite a library of books, and she'd invited him to go through a few of the boxes.

He had selected a few titles that looked interesting and some he thought may interest Sarah Ann as well.

"I'd like to call Lenore now," Sarah Ann said suddenly.

Allen handed the phone to her, and she dialed. Sarah Ann could hear the phone ring and then a voice say hello. It was a young male voice, and she realized it had to be her younger brother, one she hadn't know she had 48 hours before.

"Hello, is Lenore available?" Her voice sounded much bolder than the first time she'd called.

"I will let her know she has a call," the man replied politely, "May I ask who is calling, please?"

"Yes, it is Sarah Ann Gingerich."

"Hold on please." She heard the phone being set down and then silence.

Lenore was organizing her closet when she heard the phone ring. She assumed it was a call for one of the boys and hoped if important the caller would leave a message.

Nicholas called to her at the top of the stairs and she thanked him and picked up the extension by the bed.

"This is Lenore," she said in a friendly tone.

"Hi Lenore, this is Sarah Ann."

Lenore's heart jumped at the sound of her daughter's voice.

"Sarah Ann, I am so glad you called!

"I am calling to tell you that I had twins," Sarah Ann told her happily.

"Twins, how exciting!" Lenore said, the realization sinking in that she was now a grandmother.

Sarah Ann told her about the labor, and Lenore asked her which hospital she was at so she could send flowers. She sensed Sarah Ann hesitating.

"I have something I need to tell you," Sarah Ann said.

Lenore sat in shock as she listened to everything Sarah Ann had to tell her.

"I really do want to come see you," Lenore insisted when she'd finally finished.

"I'd love to meet you, too," Sarah Ann said.

Sarah Ann didn't know but her mother's mind was already spinning with possibilities of how she could help her newly found daughter and family.

What she had not told Sarah Ann yet was who she was married to and it was only a matter of calling Jonathan and explaining it all to him. But by doing that she would have to expose the secret she'd carried all those years. She did know however it was time and mentally prepared herself for the talk they'd be having.

Lenore immediately went online and booked an airline ticket to Springfield. She would have a two-hour drive to where Sarah Ann and Allen were staying.

She suddenly thought that she really didn't know if this was her daughter or not, and it could be some impostor. Her mind went wild with ideas, like maybe Jonathan with an extreme plan to rid himself of her. She shook her head and told herself to stop being silly. Whoever the people were on the phone, if they were not who they claimed to be, they should win the highest award given for acting.

She went back upstairs, and after brushing her teeth lay down in the large bed that had at one time not seemed so big. There was a time when she and Jonathan lay close together, and she'd often wake to find his arm thrown across her. But that was a long time ago, and now they both stayed on their own sides of the bed with a huge expanse between them.

She remembered to set her alarm and willed her brain to still enough so she could fall asleep.

The last thing she remembered thinking before drifting off to sleep was that she was a grandmother.

She wasn't sure if she felt ready for the role, but she was willing to try.

The alarm clock was an unfamiliar sound since after years of getting up at six she had trained herself to not need a clock. It startled her, and for a moment she didn't know what it was. Then reality set in, and she sat upright in bed. She turned off the alarm and thought of the long day ahead of her. Getting out of bed, she quickly took a shower and prepared herself for her day.

What does one wear that is comfortable when traveling, yet nice enough for most occasions? She settled on dark gray knit pants, stretchy enough to be comfortable and yet dressy enough to look presentable. She added a dark red sweater and put on some diamond stud earrings that were a gift from Jonathan for fifteen years of marriage. She looked through her many chains that she had accumulated over the years and settled on a Charter Club black band with a large silver circle dangling from the front. It was simple yet elegant, and she felt pleased with her choice. She quickly applied her makeup.

Her shoulder-length light brown hair had just been cut, and she was glad that she'd not canceled the appointment like she had felt tempted to do. The highlights complimented her high cheekbones. She knew that unlike most women who felt they had lost the best years of their life at forty, she had never looked better than she did now. She settled for a black, just over the ankle-high boots with a moderate heel.

Lenore hurriedly left a note for the boys telling them how much she loved them, and she'd be calling to check up on them. She was on her way out with a light coat when she suddenly remembered it would be cold where she was going and went back upstairs for a heavy coat. Finally, she felt confident she wasn't forgetting anything and was backing out of her garage.

Somehow the rift between her and Jonathan could be repaired. It wasn't until then that she realized she wanted back what they once had. Maybe now that she finally had Sarah Ann in her life she could allow herself to be loved. She, of all people knew her own issues and she also knew what the solutions were. Lenore told people every day how to cope and what to do in similar situations. It wasn't as easy doing it yourself as it was telling others how to do it, and she often felt like a hypocrite letting them believe that her life must be perfect. It had to be the right way, after all she was handing out all the high paid advice. Arriving at the airport parking area, she left her car with a valet and took the shuttle to the airport.

*****

Sarah Ann could barely contain her excitement and thought the evening would never end.

She tried to read but couldn't concentrate and kept finding herself turning back a page she had read without seeing. She wondered how it was possible that your eyes could read what your mind wasn't absorbing.

Sarah Ann suddenly broke the silence. "Do you know what scares me most of all?"

"No I don't, but tell me," Allen said in a caring tone.

"I am afraid that Lenore has expectations, and I will somehow disappoint her."

"How could you possibly disappoint her?"

"What if I look like my real father and she hates him or I do or say something wrong that she will not like," she said, sounding like she was about to cry any second.

"I think she'll take one look at you and see how wonderful you are, the same way I always see you," Allen said. "Look Sarah Ann, I am sure what you are feeling is minor compared to what she feels. She gave you up and regardless of whatever circumstances that prevented her from keeping you, she knows you are the one who would be feeling rejection."

"But right now, I don't even care about that; I keep

trying to tell myself it's the future that matters."

"But sometimes it takes understanding the past to be able to have happiness in the future," Allen said thoughtfully.

She appreciated how Allen always had the right words to say that would make her feel better. He was an amazing man, and she wanted to have a lifetime to show him how much he mattered to her.

Sarah Ann woke the next morning and lay in bed for a while listening to Allen breathe beside her. It was a comforting sound, and she still kept reminding herself she wasn't alone anymore. She wouldn't need to give up the baby. "Or babies," she thought with a smile.

She was uncertain how to feel about Will and Malinda. They had done a very nice thing years ago by rescuing a baby, but they had not done her any favors by not just abandoning her at some police station or somewhere safe. They had however, shown her kindness and she had a good home. They had never been overly affectionate and she wondered if the guilt they carried hadn't somehow prevented that from happening.

She eased herself out of bed being careful not to wake Allen. She decided to take a shower and get herself dressed. He was awake when she returned from the shower a half hour later, fully dressed but her hair was still damp.

"Good morning," he said, his voice rough from sleep.

"Wake up Sleepyhead!" she chimed. The excitement of the day lay before her, and the shower had rejuvenated her spirit.

"She'll be here in an hour and a half."

"Are you okay?" he asked.

"Yes, I am; I've waited a long time for this," Sarah Ann said with determination.

Chapter 24

Lenore found the general store and parked in front of the entrance.

She opened the car door and as she made her way to the front door, she once again fought back the question that had pounded in her head all day yesterday, "What if she doesn't like me?"

Lenore took a deep breath and knocked. A tall, good looking young man of about 25 opened the door. He smiled at her kindly and spoke. "Hello, please come in. holding the door open for her to enter."

"Sarah Ann is in the bedroom with the babies. I'll take you to her."

She stepped inside the room and there she was, a beautiful smile, standing there with a shine in her eyes. She saw that the shine was tears shimmering beneath the surface.

She smiled at her and said, "Sarah Ann, I am Lenore Collins. I have waited a long time for this moment. You look so much like what I imagined and even more. You are so beautiful."

Sarah Ann choked a bit and said, "I never really had a picture of what you'd look like in my head, but you are beautiful yourself."

"May I hug you?" Lenore asked cautiously. Sarah Ann nodded and they both hugged, gently at first and then harder. Both of them were crying when they separated.

"I just want to look at you," Lenore said sniffling.

Allen was making tea, giving them some time alone.

Sarah Ann laughed but ended in a sob, "I am so glad we found each other."

"Here are the babies," She proudly showed them to her mother and explained which was who.

Lenore gushed over them. Sitting in a chair, holding one in each arm.

Just then baby Lawrence began to cry and Sarah Ann attended to him.

Allen brought in cups of tea and took Lena Rose from Lenore.

"You have two brothers," Lenore told Sarah Ann. Nicolas is seventeen, and Alexander is fifteen. I have a picture of them. Let me show you." She reached for her purse and pulling a photo out of her wallet showed it to Sarah Ann.

Allen sat down next to Sarah Ann and she showed him the picture.

"May I ask what your life was like?" Lenore asked Sarah Ann as she was carefully putting the photo back in her purse.

Sarah Ann hesitated then said, "It was fine for the most part, but the last five years have been difficult for me. Their death was hard enough, but finding out they lied to me all those years was the worst."

"What do you mean they lied to you?"

Allen said, "Why don't you start at the beginning, Sarah Ann, and tell her everything. How you grew up with the feeling that someone was after your family."

Lenore's eyes grew large as she looked from Allen to Sarah Ann. "Yes, if you don't mind, please start from the very beginning. I know you had told me part of it on the phone, but I'd really like hearing the whole story.

So Sarah Ann told her everything, adding a few more details that Allen had not heard before. She told them how she spent so much of her life feeling something wasn't quite right, but whenever she would hint about it to Will and Malinda, they would just laugh it off. She grew teary when she talked about how she had found them and Kaitlyn lying in pools of blood.

Talking about all her memories made her tired and when she finally had spilled everything about herself that she could remember, she was drained of all emotion and energy.

Lenore sat stunned. Everything she had believed all those years had not been true at all and the promises made to her that her baby would have a warm loving home with pets and all the things that came along with a perfect family. She had believed and bought the whole nine yards that had been peddled to her.

"I am so sorry, Sarah Ann, that I gave you up to a home like that."

"They really were good to me. I know they may have lied about a lot of things, but at least they weren't unkind to me."

Lenore asked a few more questions about the video Will and Malinda had left for Sarah Ann.

Allen went to get her jewelry box and came back handing it to Sarah Ann. She took out the video and lifting out a false bottom, took out the computer files that

Will had copied so long ago.

"They don't look like anything we still use today," Allen said. "Do you think they can get information from these?"

"Yes, they can," Lenore said. "The FBI will have any equipment needed to withdraw any information that is on these." She stopped and was looking at a picture that Sarah Ann had removed when she took out the false bottom. She picked it up looking at it carefully.

"Who is this?" she asked Sarah Ann holding up the picture, a strange expression on her face.

"That is Will and Malinda, my adopted parents," Sarah Ann said. "I guess you wouldn't know who they are."

"Sarah Ann, this is the lady I gave you to. She is the one who told me you would be having all those things I was promised. She was the one who sat with me while you were born."

Lenore's face was white with shock and looked like she'd been struck across the face. Then it turned red as she felt a sudden fury at the injustice that she and Sarah Ann had endured.

"My husband is a foreign diplomat. Before that he had a position with the FBI. He knows all the right people in the right places. I am sure once they question the two men from the cabin, they'll find out who is behind all this."

Lenore immediately called Jonathan. It was the second time they'd spoken in 24 hours, and she felt some of the old feelings return. She sensed he felt the same. She told them that everything was already being worked out. Someone was being sent out immediately to pick up the files and the video tape of Will and Malinda's confession to Sarah Ann.

"Are you ready to answer questions for the FBI?" She asked Sarah Ann. "I will be happy to do whatever I can." Sarah Ann willingly agreed.

Sarah Ann burst into tears when the reality sank in that she may no longer need to be afraid.

Never again would she need to fear that someone would suddenly appear out of nowhere to take her life like they had her parents. Allen echoed his relief as well.

Two FBI agents came later that afternoon and Sarah Ann patiently answered all their questions and gave them all the information she could remember. They left taking with them all the information Will and Malinda had made available.

Late afternoon the next day a tall well-dressed man in a dark suit came striding in with Alice. She brought him back to them and Allen saw him first and noted how he commanded respect.

Lenore looked up jumping to her feet. She embraced him. "Jonathan, meet Allen, my new son-in-law."

"Hello Jonathan, it's very nice meeting you," he said warmly, his handshake strong and sure.

Allen liked him immediately. He felt a bit in awe of him though and hoped it didn't show.

Lenore showed Jonathan the babies, and Lena Rose opened her mouth in a perfect "o" and yawned.

Allen felt such a sense of pride as he watched them. Relief swept over him at the reality of knowing they never had to fear for their lives again. No one would be searching to do them harm again.

He was ready to go back to his quiet Amish life. He hoped Sarah Ann felt the same.

Lenore had exclaimed upon finding out Sarah Ann had been living among the Amish. They had answered lots of questions about Amish life the best they could.

Allen's head spun at how quickly everything had taken place. With a few phone calls made by Jonathan, their lives had drastically changed.

The men from the cabin had been questioned and had told everything they knew. With the added evidence from Will and Malinda the FBI had enough to take the steps needed to make the necessary arrests.

It was later that evening. Lenore and Jonathan had gone to their hotel.

"Sarah Ann, I've been thinking." Allen began hesitantly.

"Yes?" she questioned him softly. They'd been lying in bed, and he could tell by her breathing she still lay awake.

"I want my quiet Amish life back. I was hoping you felt the same way. The life we had before all this began."

Sarah Ann let out a long sigh. "I have been missing it as well. I'm glad you feel the same. But of course it won't quite be the same again, now that we have the twins."

"It will be so much better," Allen said happily. I can hardly wait to find out."

Sarah Ann heartily agreed.

Epilogue

Allen kept his word and visited Mr. Dolan at the hospital the very next day. He would make a full recovery, and when Allen told him how grateful they were for everything, he brushed it off as if it were nothing but all in a day's work.

Allen remembered what Alice had told them, and though Mr. Dolan said nothing, it helped knowing the reason why he had gone to such lengths to help them.

Alice Greenway refused to take any payment for anything she'd done for Allen and Sarah Ann. Any attempt at offers of money she'd refused. It was difficult for them to accept and they had discussed a way of giving back to her that she would find acceptable. The car Allen had purchased would no longer be of any purpose to them now they would be going back to the Amish life so they presented it to her.

Allen explained that had she not offered them the garage on that fateful night, the men would have stopped at the stop sign and most assuredly seen their car parked outside.

Alice shuddered at the thought of how things could have turned out and with a little persuasion graciously accepted the gift of the vehicle.

She made them promise to come back some time to visit.

Lenore had discovered what a marvelous thing it was to be able to receive love. All those years of hiding the secret of Sarah Ann from Jonathan had closed off her heart to receive love.

She was amazed at how differently Jonathan had received the news than she had envisioned. They both agreed to take marriage counseling and once again get back what they once had. But this time with no secrets. Lenore promised Sarah Ann that she would come visit them in Michigan.

The taxi drove in the driveway and stopped at the neatly shoveled walkway leading into the side entryway.

Allen and Sarah Ann each picked up a baby and walked up the sidewalk. The door opened and Amanda stood eagerly in the doorway waiting to fill her arms with the babies. She greeted them both with tears in her eyes and stepped aside so they could enter the warm kitchen. Dan stood just inside and as Allen handed a baby to Amanda turned to his father.

Dan hugged him and said in a broken voice, "Welcome home, son!"

ABOUT THE AUTHORS

Samuel Byler was born and raised in the Amish community of Geauga County, Ohio. Born into a large Amish family, he attended the school depicted on the cover. He left the Amish at the age of 19 and shortly after joined a Mennonite church where he met his wife of 21 years. They currently live in Phoenix, Arizona, and have two daughters.

Linda Byler-Sortor was raised Mennonite in Burton, Ohio. She spent lots of time with her old order Amish grandparents who would dress her in Amish clothes. She also learned the language at a very young age. Her family moved to Phoenix in 1969, where she met Randy, her husband of 40 years. They have lived in Black Canyon City, Arizona, for 30 years, and have three children and four grandchildren.

Made in the USA
San Bernardino, CA
10 January 2014